Needing Nita

Needing Nita

SERVE AND PROTECT NOVELLA

NORAH WILSON

Needing Nita

Copyright © 2010 Norah Wilson

Published by Norah Wilson

Cover by Kim Killion, Hot Damn Designs

Book design by Michael Hale, Hale Author Services

ISBN: 978-0-9878037-5-7

Chapter 1

"So, what's the story?"

Nita Reynolds glanced up at her law partner, Brad Knopfler, who stood framed in her doorway, without really seeing him.

Brain tumor. A couple of bad headaches, and now they said she had a tumor in her head. Just like her father. God, she'd only had that MRI because her mother had hounded her within an inch of her life to ask for it. Neuro-imaging was *not* the medical community's usual first response to a complaint of migraine with aura, and she'd felt like a major hypochondriac even asking her doctor about it.

"Nita?"

She blinked. *Shit.* "Sorry, Brad, what was that?"

Taking her question as an invitation, he crossed the plush carpet to settle in one of the leather armchairs opposite her desk. "Your meeting with the Crown Prosecutor this morning," he prompted, loosening his tie and lounging back in the chair. "How'd it go?"

Better than the visit with my doctor right after that.

"Good." When that came out as little more than a croak, she cleared her throat. "It was good. I talked her down from indictable to summary offence."

Brad lifted an eyebrow. "Good job. That'll save your guy four or five years, if he's convicted."

"Yeah, and there's a pretty good chance he will be."

"Hey, are you okay, Nita? You look a little ... I don't know. Wiped."

Wiped? Try *dying.*

She bit back on a bubble of laughter that threatened to erupt. Gawd, if she laughed now, she'd start crying.

"You know what? I *am* tired." She closed the file she'd been staring at for the past half hour. "I think I'm gonna play hooky and go home."

"Nita, Nita, Nita." Brad shook his head sadly. "It's four o'clock in the afternoon. That hardly qualifies. Hooky is when you call the office whilst tangled with your lover who is nibbling you in places that make your voice go husky, thereby lending you some credibility when you plead swine flu or bubonic plague or something."

At his words, a mental image sprang to life. Specifically, the image of Detective Craig Walker's hulking length sprawled on her five-hundred-dollar Egyptian cotton sheets, and her own body sprawled atop his .... .

Suddenly, her heart beat faster. And not at the mental image alone. She'd conjured it too often in these past few months for it to have *that* dramatic an effect. No, her heart beat faster at the idea taking root in her mind. The mind that could be lost to her all too soon, like her father's was after his first surgery. But it wasn't lost yet. She still had full mental capacity, full motor function. Full control of her life, at least for the immediate future.

Time to put it to good use.

She stood, smiling for the first time since leaving Dr. Woodbridge's office. "You know what? You're right again, Brad. You're absolutely right."

Grabbing her purse, she strode out.

⚜

Detective Craig Walker massaged his forehead as he listened to his aunt's friend's mother rant about the graffiti artist who'd been tagging abandoned buildings in her neighborhood in the decaying west end of Fredericton.

"I'll ask patrol to look into that, ma'am," he interjected, when it appeared she was winding down. Unfortunately, that only served to rev her up, as she interpreted his response to mean the police department did not concern itself with vandalism. He switched the receiver to the other ear and slouched back in his chair, resigned to listening a while longer.

Frankly, he'd driven through that neighborhood the other day and thought the graffiti was an improvement. And for once, he could actually approve the messages, which were clearly the work of environmental activists rather than the usual gang-related crap. *Vegan* environmental activists, judging by the two-buildings-wide *Stop feeding cows; start feeding people* message. But his favorite was the one with the beautiful, amazingly detailed rendition of the earth with the caption beneath: *Earth. Pass it on.*

"I understand your concern, Mrs. Brewer," he said when she paused again for breath. "But I'm assigned to Major Crimes, and my Sergeant would kick my butt if I took time away for something like this. I've had two serious new cases just today, and dozens more getting colder by the minute. The best I can do in the circumstances is pass your concerns along to patrol, who *will* look into it. If Aunt Gena herself called me, I'd have to give her the same answer."

That wasn't strictly true. He couldn't think of much he wouldn't do for Aunt Gena, if she asked him. But the rest of it was true, including the grinding workload. And with the fiscal belt tightening undertaken by the newly-elected mayor, the manpower additions they'd been counting on weren't likely to materialize.

After a few more assurances, he managed to get Mrs. Brewer off the line. A quick call to patrol/community policing, and the whole thing was someone else's problem.

Too bad he couldn't slough off his personal irritations so easily. Ray Morgan, a colleague in Major Crimes, was trying to set him up with his wife's friend from the newspaper. Or rather, Ray's wife Grace was trying to set him up. What was so hard to grasp about 'not interested in a relationship'? These people who were so damned happy were a pain in the ass.

And on the other side of the spectrum, he kept having to stave off Denis Dallaire. Newly divorced, Dallaire was hitting the bars again, and couldn't seem to grasp that every single guy didn't want to be out there chasing skirts every freaking night. The thing was, Craig had caught his share. Now, it just seemed more trouble than it was worth, which depressed the hell out of him. He was only 34, for chrissakes. A healthy 34-year-old man should want to be out there, shouldn't he? It was almost enough to make him take Denis up on the challenge.

But nah. Too much effort. Not so much in the chase, but in the extrication afterward.

And yeah, the vague emptiness it left him with. Not that he'd ever admit to it. At least not anywhere within earshot of Ray Morgan. There'd be no stopping Grace's matchmaking.

He'd just gotten back into the flow of his arrest report when his phone rang again. "Walker."

"Detective, it's Nita Reynolds."

He'd straightened in his chair even before she identified herself. He'd have recognized that voice anywhere. Confident, controlled, self-contained, but with an underlying hint of heat that was all the sexier for its subtlety. Much the way she looked.

"Ah, Ms. Reynolds," he said, pushing down the jumbled mixture of feelings she always managed to evoke. "Let me guess. You're representing the enterprising Edward Rayburn, who set out to find a buyer for his girlfriend's daughter while said child's meth-addicted mother sits out a jail term."

"I think you mean he *stands accused* of trying to sell the child," she corrected. "But no, I don't represent him. I was calling—"

"Of course! Gordon Bohner. I wondered who he'd find to represent him." The thought of what Bohner had done to his own mother to extract enough money for his next fix hardened his voice. "Your mother must be proud of you, Nita."

She snorted. "I don't think she ever got over her disappointment when I left Highpriced & Pompous to do Legal Aid work. And I'm not even going to ask what Mr. Bohner did."

He grinned at her use of the nickname for the multi-province mega-firm Hightower Ponder. "Don't you mean you won't ask what Mr. Bohner *stands accused* of doing?"

She made a sound, but he couldn't tell whether it was an exasperated sigh or a stifled laugh.

"God, I must be crazy," she said.

This time, he definitely detected laughter in her voice. And in that moment, he knew she wasn't calling about anyone's case. The realization sent a bolt straight to his groin. He glanced up at fellow detective Sean Casey, who sat two desks over in the detective's bullpen. Casey appeared to be engrossed in reading a file, but Craig angled his chair away from his colleague.

"I wouldn't say that," he said. "You had the good judgment to call me, after all."

"Good judgment?" She laughed again. "That remains to be seen."

He waited. Pointedly. He could have waded in there, helped her out, but dammit, why should he? He'd done the asking last time. Two times, actually. The first time, he got a polite turndown. He would never have asked again, except all the signals were still there, in flashing neon. When she turned him down the second time, she'd made it clear she didn't date cops. Period.

"I was wondering if you'd like to go to dinner with me tonight. My treat. I thought maybe Soloman's."

Soloman's. Pricey, but they had the best steak and seafood in town. They also had a relaxed enough atmosphere and dress code to attract regular Joes like him once in a while. And more significantly, Soloman's was a two-, maybe three-block walk from Nita Reynolds' downtown condo apartment. The thought sent another jolt below the belt. *Settle down, boy.*

"To be completely clear, are we talking about a date here?"

"Yes." One word, but it managed to sound strangled.

He leaned back his chair, feeling in control. A strange sensation indeed when it came to this woman. And probably short-lived, so he should enjoy it.

Apparently, he must have enjoyed it a little too long, because her voice was a little testier when she spoke again. "What? Have I stunned you into silence? Shocked you with my forwardness, maybe?"

"Nah, I was just searching for the weather report from hell. I'm guessing it must have frozen over down there."

"Very funny."

"What about your no cops rule?"

"Some rules are meant to be broken, Detective. I know you of all people would subscribe to that notion."

"Given how often I land myself in hot water with the brass, you mean?"

She made no reply.

"No comment?" he prodded.

"Sorry," she said politely, "I was letting the record speak."

He laughed. "Okay, it's a date. I'll meet you there." After a few beats of silence, he added, "What time?"

"Seven?"

"Perfect."

"One last thing, Detective . . . ."

"What's that?"

"Come prepared."

He heard her disconnect, but still he sat there with the receiver in hand, her words echoing in his mind. *Come prepared.* The dial tone kicked in, and he hung up.

Jesus. He was sitting in the middle of the bullpen with a hard-on. Suddenly, he didn't feel so in control.

꧁꧂

Nita resisted the urge to pull her compact out of her purse and check her lipstick. It was perfect when she'd applied it, and it was still perfect. For what she'd paid for it, it wouldn't dare smudge. And dammit, she looked good in her new DKNY tank dress, cute denim jacket and with calf-hugging leather boots. Hot without being too over-the-top, man-hunting slutty.

Or was it? Maybe the boots were too much.

Argh! Stupid to be nervous. It would be better when he actually got here.

Not that he was late. She'd come early to get away from her silent apartment, hoping that the buzz of conversation and the discreet bustle of the wait staff would distract her. Plus she'd wanted to be in place first to establish some kind of . . . what? — ownership? — control? . . . of this piece of recklessness she was about to embark on.

Drink. Now.

She picked up her wine, but instead of gulping it nervously, she forced herself to slow down and appreciate it. She swirled it in its glass, admiring its legginess a moment before inhaling its bouquet. Lovely. She'd bypassed the subtle sophistication of her usual French favorite and picked a lively Australian Shiraz. Lush and peppery, it was perfect for her mood. She took a sip, savoring the dominant blackberry flavor and the feel of the tannins in her mouth.

"Am I late?"

Dammit. She'd wanted to see his entrance, watch him cross the room. She glanced up and smiled. "Not at all." Their gazes collided, and her pulse leapt like she'd touched a live wire. Oh, Christmas! What had she invited? He was so big, so raw, so masculine. "Have a seat."

He did, and the hovering waiter moved in on him immediately. He glanced at her wine, then ordered a beer.

"You look beautiful," he said when the waiter left. The frank appreciation in his ridiculously blue eyes echoed the sentiment.

"Thank you." She inclined her head in acknowledgement. "You look pretty good yourself."

That was the understatement of the year. Their previous encounters had pretty much been confined to the courtroom or the stationhouse, so she knew he cut an imposing, if slightly incongruous, figure in a suit. But tonight he wore a tan-colored ultrasuede sport coat over an oatmeal colored sweater with a very fine looking pair of denims in a shade of blue almost as piercing as his eyes. Her hands itched already for the tactile sensation of those fabrics. And as for what lay beneath . . . .

She didn't realize how hungrily she was staring until her eyes completed the journey up his chest, past his strong neck to the brutally hard planes of his face and met his gaze. Oh, yikes!

"Are you hungry?" she asked.

He lifted an eyebrow. "For what's on the menu, you mean?"

"Yes."

"Depends. Is there something else on offer?"

She felt a blush climbing her neck, but held his gaze. "Most definitely."

He stood abruptly, jarring the table and nearly toppling her wine. Flagging down a passing waiter, he said, "The lady's not feeling well." He pulled out his wallet and pressed some bills into the waiter's hand. "For the drinks."

She stood and he was at her side instantly with a solicitous hand at her back. As they wended their way among the tables to the exit, she felt the burn of that touch through her clothes. Come to that, she felt his body heat reaching out to her. God, he was a blast furnace. She couldn't wait to get her hands on him.

"Your car or mine?" he asked when they hit the street.

"My place is just a few blocks away. Why don't we walk it?"

"Okay, but first I have to do this." He pulled her into the alley between the restaurant and the art gallery next door, pushed her up against the cool brick of the building and kissed her.

It was not a searching, tentative kiss. It was urgent and fiercely demanding, as were the hands that skimmed down her shoulders to her hips. Her blood leapt in response, and she met his mouth with demands of her own. Her hands found their way under his jacket, then under his sweater. His skin was just as hot as she knew it would be, but the muscle beneath was so much more solid than she'd imagined. Like no man she'd ever touched.

She slid her arms around him, and he made an approving sound against her mouth. And when she slid her hands down to test his butt through the denim of his jeans, he surged against her thrillingly, once. Then he pulled back, the cool of the August evening replacing his warmth.

"Baby, we gotta get this off the streets. C'mon." He tugged her back onto the sidewalk and wrapped one arm around her shoulders. "Lead the way."

Chapter 2

CRAIG HAD DIED AND gone to heaven. That could be the only explanation. Nita Reynolds — the woman who'd turned him down cold on two occasions — had called him out of the blue for a dinner date. Then she'd taken one look at him and decided to jump straight to dessert. It was too good to be true.

Not that he couldn't walk into plenty of bars and walk right back out with an attractive woman on his arm. But not a woman like Nita. She wasn't into cops, uniformed or otherwise. Hell, if there was such a thing as an *anti*-badge bunny, she was it. Nor would he have said she was into casual sex. She was way too discriminating. Way too self-contained.

So why him? And why now?

On his way to the restaurant, he'd begun to think she was planning to play him. He didn't know how or why, but concluded that had to be it. She knew she turned his crank. She'd buy him dinner, flirt with him, maybe kiss him goodnight at the end of the evening and dangle the possibility of another date, all in aid of softening him up for some unknown purpose that would reveal itself in the fullness of time. But one look at her tonight and those thoughts flew out the window.

That she was a natural actor, he had no doubt. She was a trial lawyer, after all. But she was no Meryl Streep. She flat out wanted him as much as he wanted her.

And he intended they both get what they wanted.

"This one."

She directed him to the five-story brownstone he'd already recognized as hers, though she'd probably be freaked if she knew. Then he'd have to explain that he'd been on his way into Soloman's one night just as she was leaving. She'd hurried off without seeing him, but as he watched, a man fell in step behind her. Unable to just shrug and go on in to enjoy the rare steak he'd earned after pulling a double shift, he wound up following the follower. As it turned out, she wasn't being stalked. The man veered off, dashed up a walkway and entered a building. Craig had stopped tailing her, but he was still watching when she turned up her own walkway and entered the brownstone. In fact, he was still watching when he saw lights came on way up on the fifth floor. He'd be very surprised if the unit on the front left side wasn't hers.

They climbed the steps together. Her hand trembled, he saw, as she entered the code to unlock the door. Moving close behind her, he slid an arm around her waist and pulled her luscious derriere into contact with his stiffening erection. She went limp, leaning back against him. Grinning, he closed his hand over hers, turned the knob and pushed the door open.

They all but fell inside.

"The elevator," she said, pulling him to the other side of the small, empty foyer. The speed with which she moved was gratifying.

"No doorman?"

"No."

They stepped into the elevator, which looked altogether too modern for the old building. "Fast elevator?"

"Very," she said, hitting the button for the fifth floor.

"Too bad." He crowded her up against a mirrored wall of the elevator, skimming the sides of her breasts with his hands. "These mirrors are great." He nipped at her mouth. "I'd love to lift that sexy dress and go down on you right here while you watched us."

She made a mewling noise against his lips, which made him smile. Then the elevator lurched to a stop. He lifted his head. They appeared to be between the fourth and fifth floors. "*You* did that?"

She smiled the most carnal smile he'd ever seen. "Whoops."

Hot damn. He'd intended that comment to heighten her excitement, never dreaming she'd call him on it. His own smile broadened. "No security camera?" he asked, looking over his shoulder.

"Just in the foyer."

"No alarm downstairs when the elevator stops?"

"I wouldn't know."

"Better not waste time, then, huh?"

She touched her tongue to her upper lip. "Better not."

He slid to his knees before her. She leaned back against the wall, bracing her backside on a wide wooden rail that he hoped was as functional as it was decorative. He skimmed his hands up her bare legs and under her skirt until he hooked her thong panties and drew them down. She lifted one booted foot obligingly and then the other. Sliding the scrap of black lace into his pocket, he pushed her dress up and urged her thighs apart.

And caught his breath.

God, she was lovely. And her scent … . He wished he could take all day. Some things just shouldn't be rushed, and this most intimate of acts was one of them. But they'd stalled the elevator, so time was of the essence. It was a trade-off he could live with.

"Craig?"

Ah, there it was, his name on her lips at last. He'd thought she was still going to be calling him 'Detective' when he was inside her.

"Hold this," he ordered, pushing the bunched-up skirt against her belly. When she complied, he urged her legs further apart and used his hands to part the already swollen lips of her sex. "Beautiful."

She shuddered at the mere tickle of his breath, making him smile again.

He leaned in and stroked her with the flat of his tongue, and she shuddered again. "Are you watching us?"

"God, yes!"

Then there were no more words — he because his mouth was otherwise occupied, and she because she seemed to have lost the power of intelligible speech. When he felt her reaching for release minutes later, he added his fingers to the mix, breaching her slick channel. She came almost immediately. A strangled sob escaped her even as her inner muscles contracted powerfully around his fingers.

When she stopped shaking, he climbed to his feet. "I really like your elevator."

She laughed, brushing her dark hair back from her face. "Riding it will never be the same."

"Good." He pulled her too him and kissed her once, hard, then put her away. Any more contact than that, and this elevator would be stalled a helluva lot longer. "Let me see if I can get this contraption going again."

※

Nita collected herself while he restarted the elevator. No small feat, standing pantiless in her elevator with the combined tastes of Craig Walker and her own fulfillment on her lips. Dear Lord, that was the wildest thing she'd ever done, and definitely the hottest! Why hadn't she gotten him in bed six months ago?

Because you thought you had a career to protect. Men inevitably boasted of their conquests, and being a criminal defense lawyer, she'd be massively boast-worthy around the stationhouse. And if that happened, she'd lose face with these guys. And gals. Female cops would be even more brutal in their judgment.

And yes, maybe because she also had a heart to protect. She'd never met a man who could see into her like this one could. All he had to do was lock those eyes on her, and she felt like her deepest secrets were right there to be exposed.

And he was a big man in more ways than one. When he lost a round in court, which wasn't often, he could let it go, unlike most of Fredericton's finest. Instead of shooting her lethal looks, he'd just shrug, confident that if her client really was a bad guy, he'd have another chance to put him away.

No, he was altogether too attractive a package. But at the same time, he scared the hell out of her. He could swallow her up, if she gave him a chance. And no doubt he'd spit her back out when he was finished with her.

Of course, that was back when she thought she had a future to worry about.

She caught herself before she could slide further into self-pity. There'd be none of that tonight. Tonight was about seizing the moment and living it to the fullest. It was about completely filling her senses.

"Got it," he announced.

The elevator lurched back into motion for a few seconds before stopping at the fifth floor. To Nita's relief, the doors opened to an empty hallway, sparing them from facing Mr. Barnett with the unmistakable smell of sex wafting off them.

She dug out her key and led the way to her apartment. Again, she felt him close behind her as she slotted her key in the door, but this time she managed to get it open under her own steam. He closed the door behind them and when she turned, he took her into his arms.

"Damn, I'm so ready for you," he murmured against her ear.

Just like that, she was ready again, too. Her brain was full of signals transmitted by her breasts, by her belly, her skin. Every bit of her that came into contact with him screamed for more contact. For skin to skin contact. She pushed her hands beneath his jacket. "Get this off!"

He shrugged out of it. She heard it hit the floor and his arms came back around her.

"Better?"

"Much." She slid her hands under his sweater, pushing it up. "But it would be better yet if you got this off, too."

He stepped back and pulled the sweater over his head, tossing it to the floor.

Nita's mouth went dry. She was no stranger to nicely toned chests, but they usually belonged to spare, compact men. The kind of safe men she dated. Aesthetes. Intellectuals. But Craig Walker's chest ... . She'd had a good idea he'd be heavily muscled; even the most civilized suit couldn't hide that. But, oh God, he was so much more. And not gym-honed show muscles. These muscles meant business.

"You like?"

Maybe she should have been embarrassed to be caught feasting on him so openly, but after what just transpired in her elevator, and considering what was yet to come, maidenly vapors seemed pointless. "You're not what I'm used to."

"Too much brawn?"

"Too much everything." She placed a hand in the center of his chest, where she felt his heart pounding as strongly as her own. "And the way I feel tonight, that might be just enough."

Before she knew what he intended, he scooped her up in his arms, giving her a heart-jolting demonstration of what those muscles could do.

"Which way to the bedroom?"

"Down that hall and to the left." Her heart thundered so hard, she could hear it in her ears. Hell, he could probably hear it. Maybe even feel it.

She'd left a lamp burning by the bedside, so there was no need to fumble for light switches. She expected him to lay her on the bed and come down on her, crushing her to the mattress with his body. She wanted that desperately. Wanted him to forcibly drive every other thought from her mind with a ferocious onslaught. Instead, he set her back on her feet at the bed's edge.

"God, you're beautiful." Catching her head, he fisted his hands in her hair and kissed her. The desperate edge of hunger was still there, but this time, the demand was subdued.

He was, she realized, putting control squarely in her hands, giving her a chance to set the pace. Or maybe even to change her mind.

Oh, God, he hadn't changed *his* mind, had he?

As if sensing her disquiet, he lifted his head a fraction, still holding her face close to his.

From this distance, his blue eyes seemed to see right through to her soul.

"Why did you call me?" he said.

The question took her aback. She touched her tongue to her upper lip in a gesture she hoped would distract him. "I should think that would be obvious by now."

He smiled. "Honey, that was obvious from the first time we locked horns in the court room."

"Thank you for reminding me. It must have been obvious for the jury, too. They gave the edge to you."

"You know what I mean," he said, clearly unwilling to be deflected. "Why now? Why after all this time? Why after turning me down?"

"Because I got tired of fighting it. Because I had the most trite of epiphanies. Because life is short, and if I'm going to regret anything, I'd prefer to regret what I did, not what I didn't do." She tipped her chin up to look him in the eyes. "Is that good enough for you, Detective? Can we get on to the part where we're naked?"

It must have been good enough, because seconds later, she found herself right where she'd yearned to be a minute ago, flat on her back in the center of her bed with Craig's weight pinning her while he pillaged her mouth, her throat. And his hands! A large palm worked her right breast through her clothes, then skimmed down to grip her hip. With a groan, he moved over her, creating an unbearably delicious friction. When he started sliding down her body, her eyes snapped open? Surely he wasn't . . . .

He wasn't.

He continued south to her boots, found the slide zippers and slid them off, one at a time, tossing them on the floor. She'd shrugged part way out of her jacket by the time he dispensed with her boots, and he helped her tug it off. The dress followed, over her head, then the lacy bra beneath.

"I knew it." He sat back on his heels to look at her. "I just knew those nipples would be small and dark and just as gorgeous as the rest of you."

Lying there with him looking at her like that, she *felt* gorgeous. "I did some imagining myself, but judging from the revelation I got when you took off your shirt, I might have . . . um . . . come up short."

He laughed. "Time to find out how fertile your imagination was."

He scooted off the bed, dug a condom from the front pocket of his jeans, then shucked the jeans, underwear and all.

Nita sucked in a breath. Jutting from a nest of dark hair, his cock was . . . magnificent. Her imagination hadn't shortchanged him in the length department, but oh, baby, the girth!

And it was all hers.

She drew herself up on her elbows. "Are you going to bring that lovely thing over here, Detective, or do I have to come after it?"

He tossed her the condom. "Why don't you come and get it?"

The heat in his eyes kicked the excitement in her belly up another notch. She scooted over until she sat on the edge of the bed. Gaze locked with his, she tore the wrapper off the condom. Then she dropped her gaze to his organ. Dear God, it was a thing of beauty. And the sooner she sheathed it, the sooner he could be inside her.

But first ....

❦

Craig steeled himself for her touch. The way her eyes had saucered at the sight of him damn near snapped his control. He was way too close to the edge for his liking. So why the hell had he tossed her the condom and invited her to put it on him?

Because you're a masochist, Walker. Because it's Nita. Because you still can't believe you're here and she wants you because — oh, Jesus!

Her hands were on him now, small and soft and elegantly feminine, right down to the white tips of her French-manicured nails. His cock jerked in response, hardening to stone. Then she leaned forward. He could feel her breath on him, warm and exciting and oh, God, if only she would open those gorgeous lips and —

Ahhhh!

Even as he fantasized about it, she guided the head of his cock into her mouth, sealing her lips delicately over the glans. A tortured groan escaped him. In response, she took more of him into her mouth. For a moment, his world shrank to a few square inches, encompassing nothing more than his cock and the hot, wet section of her mouth. It was so ... damned ... good.

Oh, hell, *too* good.

"Nita!" He tangled a hand in her hair. "You have to stop, baby. I don't ... I can't ...."

She released him. "Sorry. Couldn't resist."

"I'm glad you didn't. But —"

"I know. Now come closer so we can get this thing on you."

He obliged, holding his breath as she applied the condom and rolled it down his shaft. The moment it was in place, she scooted back to the center of the bed. He followed her down, lying beside her. In a gratifying display of eagerness, she tried to pull him atop her.

"Soon, baby." She might think she was ready, but with his fuse being this short, he needed her to be more than ready.

For all her eagerness to get to the main event, when he kissed her, she subsided, apparently content to enjoy the play of lips and tongue. And for all his eagerness to get inside her, he wanted this, too. He'd fantasized about kissing that smart mouth of hers since that first day in the witness box. And a hundred times since. He poured all of that frustrated yearning into the kiss. She took it all and demanded more.

When she grew restless again, he palmed her breast, drawing a gasp from her. When he drew his fingers together to gently pinch and roll her stiffened nipple, she caught fire, straining against him.

"Please, Craig. Now."

"Soon, baby," he promised, then swooped to catch her nipple in his mouth. She whimpered once, and again when he used his teeth. Oh, Lord, that sound! It shuddered right through him. He wanted to draw it from her again and again and again. Every night. All night.

Lust hazing his brain, he rolled her under him, letting their lower bodies tangle while keeping his upper body propped above her. She splayed her legs, making a cradle for his aching cock. As her hands roamed his chest feverishly, he gazed down at her breasts, her flushed neck, her face, wanting to memorize exactly what she looked like at this moment.

"You're so beautiful."

Something flickered in her eyes. Then she closed them, shutting him out even as she slid her hands around behind him to squeeze his ass. "Please." She undulated beneath him. "I'm ready. Don't make me wait any longer."

He didn't.

He entered her slowly, carefully, gritting his teeth against the urge to seat himself fully. Still, it wrenched a sob from her. He froze. "Nita?"

"Oh, God, don't stop!"

He drew out and pushed in a little further. The hot, wet clasp of her flesh was pure madness, inviting him to let go of all restraint, but he didn't dare. She was so small, so snug ... so fucking *hot!*

Despite himself, he rocked into her a little harder.

"Yes! Yes!" She arched up, trying to take more of him.

Control gone, he surged into her, burying himself to the hilt. She cried out again, but there was no mistaking her approval. Needing no further urging, he started to move against her, fucking her with long, slow strokes, pulling out almost all the way only to push home again. For long moments, there was nothing but the sound of sex: the slap of flesh against flesh, the harshness of their breathing. His excitement rose higher, coiled tighter. When she begged for more, he gathered her close, switching to a grinding, purposeful, insistent rhythm. Beneath him, she made that whimpering sound again and angled her hips in an effort to maximize the friction against her clitoris. He thought about how she'd tasted in the elevator, how her legs had trembled when he'd licked and sucked that sweet bundle of nerves.

Ahh! Dammit, he shouldn't have gone there.

"Oh, Christ, Nita. Come on with me, baby. Come for me."

Even as he said it, he realized she didn't need any urging. She was already flying apart, her internal muscles clamping him like a vise, rippling. He let go, pumping into her mindlessly until his climax exploded.

Chapter 3

Five minutes later, Nita stood under a hot spray of water in the shower.

While other women talked about afterglow, she'd never been able to lie more than a minute in bed before needing to jump up and shower. She'd long ago stopped worrying about what that compulsion said about her and just accepted it. And it had suited the men she'd dated just fine. They usually took the opportunity to dress so they could kiss her goodbye when she emerged from the bathroom, and they both went to bed happy, each in their own homes.

But this time, with Craig Walker's muscled arm slung across her midriff and one powerful leg still tangled with hers, she hadn't wanted to pull away. She'd wanted to burrow closer. She wanted to touch his face, inhale the scent of his skin, feel the springy texture of his hair beneath her fingers. Hell, she wanted to crawl inside his skin.

Naturally, she'd immediately leapt up and headed for the bathroom.

What the hell was wrong with her?

What's wrong with you, Reynolds? You've got a tumor in your head that will probably kill you, with or without surgery, in a matter of months, and you're wondering what's wrong with you because you wanted to be close to someone for a few minutes?

No, not *someone*. Craig Walker.

A draft of cool air warned her that she wasn't alone in the bathroom any longer, so she was neither shocked nor startled when he drew back the shower curtain and stepped into the shower with her. *Yes*, she thought, stepping back to make room for him. *God, yes.*

He reached for her and she went gladly into his arms, her flesh wet and giving against the solidity of his chest. He turned them so the shower spray beat down on his back and covered her mouth with his. And there it was again. She wanted to be under him, on him. Christ, *inside* him.

She wrenched her mouth away from his. "Were you counting on getting much sleep tonight, Detective?"

His grin was lethal. "Not if I can help it."

"Good. Because I want to have you every way I can think of. I want you in every room, in every position, until we're both too sore to do it again."

He sucked in a deep breath. "Jesus, Nita."

"Does that mean you're up for it?"

He drew her hand down to his stiffened cock. "What do you think?"

She smiled. "I think we can scratch the bathroom off the list."

"The tub enclosure, at least."

❧

Six hours later, Craig lay watching Nita sleep in his arms.

She hadn't planned to fall asleep, but he'd convinced her to lie down with him while he drank some ice water, ate a slice of cold pizza, which they'd ordered at midnight, and generally recuperated from their last bout of sex.

Part of him was still expecting her to spring something on him that would explain his good fortune — a request for a highly improper favor or for confidential information on an investigation — but she'd scrupulously avoided anything work-related.

Instead, they'd exhausted the easy stuff during the earlier 'intermissions'. They both shared a love of jazz, though she leaned more toward contemporary and he more toward traditional. They now knew which three books and three albums the other would choose if they were stranded alone on a desert island, and there was actually some crossover. Her favorite actor was some guy he'd never heard of because he rarely saw movies these days, and he'd fessed up that he was still stuck on Kirstie Alley — thin, fat or in between — because she was beautiful. She detested football, hockey and basketball, but somehow had developed a love for baseball.

When the small talk petered out, she'd asked him about his family. He'd been in the process of telling her about his older sister when he realized she was sleeping, a fact that registered only when she rolled toward him and nestled her head on his shoulder.

So here he was, clinging to wakefulness. His eyes burned from lack of sleep, and his body was beyond exhausted, but no way was he going to sleep. As glorious as this night had been, these minutes with the warm, trusting weight of her tucked against his body were too precious to miss. Because as many times as they'd made love tonight, she'd never really let him hold her. Every time he tried to show her tenderness, she subtly redirected him.

Okay, maybe not so subtly. The last time, she'd ordered him to dress and wait for her in her office. She'd come in dressed in a short skirt, low-cut blouse and tall stilettos. Pen and notepad in hand, she'd offered to take dictation. Fast forward ten minutes and that red skirt was bunched up around her waist as she backed up onto his lap, taking his needy cock into her yet again. He'd swiveled the chair to face the mirror on the end wall so they could both watch him unbutton her shirt and liberate her breasts from the pushup bra. She'd moaned as he toyed with her, gently pinching her out-thrust nipples one moment, then palming her full breasts the next. Kneading, squeezing, lifting them like an offering .... Finally he had to abandon them to grip her hips as she picked up the tempo, but the image of her breasts bouncing more than made up for it.

So really, how could a guy complain? He'd have to be nuts. She'd given her body over to him completely, yielding up every ounce of passion she possessed, and she'd demanded the same from him. It was like she was worried tonight was all they had, and every sexual fantasy had to be fulfilled before some fairy godmother came along and waved a wand to take it all back.

Shit. Maybe that was it. Maybe she *was* afraid it would all be over, come morning, that he'd go on his way now that he'd had what she figured he wanted from her.

Ah, but little did she know what he wanted.

Okay, sure, little had *he* known what he wanted until five hours ago. But now he knew. She was for him and he was for her. And soon he'd make her see it.

He gathered her closer, kissed the top of her head and promptly fell asleep.

Chapter 4

NITA WOKE TO THE sound of her telephone ringing, but when she rolled toward the phone, she smacked into the solid wall of a man. Holy shit, *Craig Walker*! Memories from last night came flooding back to her. Lord, she'd fallen asleep on him. She'd just closed her eyes for a minute . . . .

The phone shrilled again. She glanced at clock. Yikes! Almost nine! It was probably Brad calling to find out where the devil she was. "The phone," she said. "Could you reach it for me?"

He picked up the receiver and handed it to her.

She pressed the receiver to her ear. "Sorry, I slept in. I'll be there in forty minutes."

"I'm afraid I'll be at the hospital doing rounds by then, but I'll be glad to make some space for you this afternoon if you want to come in, after you've heard what I have to say."

Doctor Woodbridge? "Sorry, Doc. I thought you were my law partner." The short telephone cord meant she had to lean across Craig, and he took the opportunity to settle a possessive hand on her hip. Despite her disoriented state, her pulse jumped at his touch.

"Are you feeling all right?" came the doctor's voice. "Another headache?"

"No, I'm fine." She put a hand on Craig's wandering hand to arrest it so she could concentrate. "I just ... didn't sleep much."

Craig grinned at her, drawing her attention to the sexy stubble on his face. A face that he must have shaved painstakingly last night before meeting her, judging by how smooth it had felt on her inner thighs . . . .

She realized then that Dr. Woodbridge had said something she totally missed. "I'm sorry, I'm still a little groggy. What was that?"

"I said it was understandable that you'd have trouble sleeping, but I think you'll fare better tonight after you've heard what I have to say. Nita, there was a mix up at the hospital. The scans they sent me weren't yours."

She jackknifed up. "Not mine?"

"That's exactly what I'm saying. The MRI report I showed you belonged to another unfortunate woman."

"So . . . I don't really have brain cancer, then? Is that what you're telling me? No tumor in my head?"

"I haven't seen your scan myself, but I'm assured that it's as clean as they come."

She put a hand to her head, which had begun to whirl as though she had a hangover. "I'm not dying?"

"Nita, honey, we're all dying, but in your case, not for a good long while."

"I see." *Omigod, omigod, omigod, what had she done?*

"I know this is a shock. And I'm sorry to have put you through this anxiety for no reason. I'd do anything not to have scared you like this, especially after your dad's experience. On the other hand, I'm damned glad to be giving you good news now."

"Of course."

She wasn't dying.

And she'd just done a Fredericton PD detective as fully, completely and inventively as a woman could do a man, and she was going to live to hear about it from every cop in the city. And probably every councilman and crown prosecutor and sheriff's deputy, too. A groan escaped her lips.

"Would you like to come in this afternoon? I'll have your MRI report by then and will be happy to go over it with you, if you like."

"No," she said sharply. "No, that's fine. I've got to go, Doc."

He was apologizing again for having upset her needlessly, but she passed the receiver to Craig and scuttled out of bed while he replaced it on the cradle.

"I'm late." She rushed to the closet, grabbed a robe and pulled it on over her nakedness before turning back to the man in her bed. He lay there altogether too collected and still for her liking, his eyes narrowed so she could barely see their vivid blueness. Oh, shit. This was not going to be pleasant. She rushed to fill the silence. "I forgot to set the alarm, and now I have to shower and get to work. I'd offer you breakfast, but don't really have time, and I need—"

"I can't fucking believe this."

Craig launched himself off her bed in an explosion of motion that sent her heart into her throat.

"You're going to send me off without a word about that conversation you just had? You're not even going to try to explain that?"

She fell back a step. She couldn't do this right now. She just couldn't. She needed to regroup, compose herself. "It's just that I'm already late and I have clients—"

He took a step closer, naked, angry and *oh God*, incredibly intimidating.

"It's okay, Ms. Reynolds. I think I can put the puzzle pieces together for myself. You called me because you thought you were *dying*. Am I right?"

"Yes, but—"

"Jesus Christ! What was I to you? Some kind of carnival ride you wanted to take? Something to cross off your to-do list before you went to meet the ultimate judge in the sky?" He raked a hand through his hair. "Christ, of course! That's why we had to squeeze in every fantasy you could think of. You wanted to cross them off so you could move on to skydiving or smoking opium or swimming with goddamn dolphins."

"That's not fair! The doctor only told me yesterday. I thought I was … dammit, it was an impulse."

He reached for his jeans and hauled them on. "I can't *fucking* believe this."

What was the matter with him? Why was he so angry? And what about *her*? What about her feelings? "*You* can't believe it?" Her hands fisted at her side. "If the stupid hospital hadn't made a hideous mistake, I never would have—"

"You never would have called me," he finished for her. "You never would have fucked me. I get it. Believe me." He glanced around, "Where the hell is my sweater?"

"In the foyer, I think."

He turned on his heel and left the room.

Shit.

She followed him out. His movements were short and sharp as he jammed his arms into the sweater and hauled it over his head. *Say something, Nita.*

"I'm sorry."

"I'll bet." Grabbing his jacket, he started for the door.

"Wait!"

He paused, hand on the doorknob. "What?"

"You won't ... I mean, you're not going to ... ?"

He turned to face her, his expression cold and flat. "Not going to what?"

"You won't tell anyone?"

His mouth tightened. "Don't worry. When I've been a fool, I rarely broadcast the fact."

A second later, he was gone and she was staring at her closed door.

Chapter 5

CRAIG SAT AT HIS desk, fingers on his keyboard, eyes on his monitor. But all he was seeing were pictures inside his own head. Nita Reynolds in her elevator. On her dining room table. In that hot skirt. In nothing at all.

And God help him, as she slept in his arms, warm and trusting and entirely defenseless.

How could he have fallen for her?

Because you've been halfway in love with her from the first time she tried to skewer you on the witness stand.

"Uh-oh. I think I know that look."

Ray Morgan's voice startled the hell out of him, but Craig managed not to jump out of his skin. "Dammit, Razor, someone oughta hang a bell on you."

Ray handed him a coffee. "No need. My knees are getting creakier by the year. You'll soon be able to hear me coming." Ray plunked himself down in Sean Casey's vacant chair and opened his own coffee. "So, what's the story? You're looking like a man with a woman on his mind. And not in the good way."

"Oh, Christ." Craig glanced around the empty bullpen. "That obvious?"

"The last time I saw a face like that was in my own mirror when Grace and I had that trouble last year."

That *trouble* was a Russian mob boss who'd put himself between Ray and his wife.

"You guys almost died, Razor. I don't think this compares."

"Yeah, but the almost-dying part wasn't the worst part." He leaned back in the chair and kicked his feet up on Casey's desk. "The worst part was thinking I'd lost her. And that's the look you were wearing just now."

Craig busied himself opening his coffee lid. "Again, hardly compares. You and Grace had been married for years. I'm talking one night. It's nothing."

Ray took a sip of his coffee, then put it down on the desk. "Bullshit."

"Excuse me?"

"Okay, maybe you were with her just one night, but no way a woman you've only just met messes you up like this. It's gotta be someone you've been stuck on a while. Which explains why you'd never let Grace set you up."

"No, I never let Grace set me up because I'm not interested in a relationship."

"Sorry if I'm starting to sound like a broken record, but I repeat, *bullshit*. You want a relationship, all right, but you want it with this woman, not someone Grace has in mind for you."

"Gee, thanks, Dr. Phil."

"Dr. Phil?" Razor swung his feet to the floor and sat up in the chair. "*Dr. Fucking Phil?* I could shoot you right now and be completely exonerated by the Police Commission."

Craig snorted. "You're probably right."

"Goddamn right I am." He pushed to his feet. "Enjoy your coffee."

"Ray?"

The other man stopped and turned. "Yeah?"

Shit, why was this stuff so damned hard to talk about? "You're right. I guess I *do* want a relationship. But she doesn't. She just wanted ... well, what she wanted, she got last night, shall we say."

"Are you sure about that?"

"Ahhhhh, yuh. Pretty sure. When I want to cuddle more than she does, the writing's on the wall."

"Huh."

"Huh?" Craig scowled. "What's that mean?"

"Not to generalize, but in my experience, women are all about relationships. With men, with their sisters, their parents, their friends, their co-workers. Hell, their doctors, their dog groomers and their paperboys. It just doesn't sound right that she'd do you for the sake of doing you, then cut you loose.

"No insult to your do-ability intended," he hastened to add.

Craig closed his eyes. "Okay, you can shoot me now."

"Were there extenuating circumstances? Some reason why she might want to project a different front?"

Like thinking she was dying of a brain tumor when she wasn't? Like being deathly afraid he would kiss and tell the whole precinct and half the judicial community, thereby undermining her ability to do her job? Like being able to drum up the courage to call him only when she figured it couldn't hurt her clients. Christ, he was a moron.

He opened his eyes. "Yeah, you could say that. You could definitely say that."

Ray smiled. "Well, there you go, then."

Chapter 6

NITA MANAGED TO STAVE off facing Brad until mid-afternoon, since he'd been tied up in court all morning and she'd had a client in her office when he got back. Shortly after 3:00 pm, though, she heard the chair in his office squeak. Dragging closer the file she'd been working on so half-heartedly for the past half hour, she buried her nose in it. *Busy Nita. Too busy for idle office chatter.*

"She lives."

Nita groaned inwardly. She hadn't really expected her show of busy-ness to deter her partner, but it was worth a try. *"She lives?"* She sat back, tossing her pen on the table. "I guess I must be awfully routine-bound if you write me off as dead the first time I come in an hour late."

"That's what I've been trying to tell you, sweetie." He moved into her office and settled in her leather client chair. "You look tired. In a nice way, of course."

"Of course."

His eyes narrowed as he regarded her. "In fact, if I didn't know better, I'd guess you were up all night having wild monkey sex."

She rolled her eyes. "Right. Because that's *so* me," she said, but she felt the telltale heat of a flush rising in her cheeks. *Don't notice, don't notice, don't notice.*

He noticed.

"Good God! You *did* have wild monkey sex! It's written all over your face. And frankly, on the left side of your neck, now that I look at you."

"It is not!" She lifted a horrified hand to her throat. "Is it?"

He laughed. "No, but now I know for sure what I only suspected before." He leaned back smugly. "And may I add, about time."

She covered her face with both hands and groaned. "God, I can't believe I fell for that."

"Me either. I mean, you *taught* me that little trick."

"Don't remind me." She picked up the pen she'd tossed down in resignation a moment earlier. "Now that you've ferreted out the dirty truth, get the hell out of my office, Knopfler. I've got work to do."

"Knock, knock."

Nita glanced up to see Maryanne, the firm's receptionist, framed in her doorway. Thank goodness. This would send Brad on his way. "What's up, Maryanne?"

"There's a Detective Craig Walker here to see you."

"What?" She jumped up from her chair, sending it backwards on its casters. "Did you tell him I'm here?"

"Omigod!" Brad said.

Maryanne frowned, sending Brad one of her patented disapproving looks that she seemed to reserve for him. "Of course I told him you were here. Why wouldn't I?" She turned back to Nita. "Are you on the lam or something? Dodging a summons?"

"It's him!" Brad said, oblivious of Maryanne's evil eye. "You had monkey sex with Detective Walker!"

Maryanne's eyes widened. "Nita?"

Nita sank back onto her chair. "Someone shoot me, please."

"Sorry," Brad quipped. "No sidearm. But if you ask the detective nicely . . . ."

She sighed. "Okay, both of you — *out*. Now. And Maryanne, please show Detective Walker in."

"Not necessary." The voice was Craig Walker's, and it came from her open door. "I showed myself in. I was beginning to get concerned you might rabbit on me."

Oh, God, had he heard all of that? She lifted her chin, aiming for dignity. *"Rabbit?* Is that your usual experience with a woman on the morning after, Detective?"

"Only with you." He glanced pointedly at the other occupants of the room.

Maryanne cleared her throat. "Well, then, I'll just get back to my post." Eyes wide, she sidled past Craig.

"And I'll just go next door to my office and press a drinking glass to the wall."

"Bradley!"

"What? I'm just making a point."

"Okay, point taken. We'll take this outside the office." She turned to Craig. "Detective."

He stepped back. "After you."

"My car or yours?" he asked when they reached the parking lot.

His, she deduced, was a slightly muscular looking but spacious Ford Taurus. Hers was a tiny hybrid. They'd be in each other's laps in her car. "Yours."

He led the way to his car, opening the door for her. She slipped inside and waited for him to join her.

"Look, Craig," she said, as soon as he'd slipped behind the wheel. "I'm really sorry about this morning. I guess I was a little stunned when Dr. Woodbridge dropped his bombshell. His *second* bombshell."

"So am I. Sorry about this morning, I mean. I shouldn't have stormed off like that. But before we go there, I gotta ask — what's with telling everyone back there? I thought you were worried about keeping the whole thing under wraps."

She blushed to the roots of her hair. "I didn't exactly tell anyone. Brad figured it out. I mean, not that I'd spent the night with *you*, specifically, but that I'd spent a long night with someone. Then Maryanne came in at that exact moment and announced that you were here to see me. I guess I freaked a little, and Brad put two and two together."

His mouth tightened. "I'm sorry. I wouldn't have come here to your office if I'd thought it would cause you further embarrassment."

She grimaced. "I'm not embarrassed. Well, sort of, but just because I'm not accustomed to my sex life coming up for discussion at the office. It's more —"

"You were afraid it would get around," he finished for her. "That I'd brag to the guys at the cop shop and you'd lose credibility. That ultimately, it would adversely affect your ability to defend your clients." He turned away to look straight ahead out the windscreen. "I understand. Hell, I can't even work up any righteous indignation anymore. Because to be honest, if I were ten years younger and stupider, I probably *would* have shot my mouth off first chance I got. But I haven't and I won't. But none of that alters the fact that I shouldn't have gone off on you like that."

"Don't apologize." She looked down at her hands, clasped in her lap. "You were right. I wouldn't have called you if I hadn't thought I was dying. That's the bald truth of it. You have every right to be angry."

"Maybe," he agreed. "But that's only half the reason I was angry."

She shot a look at him, but he was still facing forward. "And the other reason?"

He turned to face her, his blue eyes fiercely intent. "I was mad because I let my mind go down that road. I let myself imagine how I'd feel if you really *did* have a brain tumor, if you really were dying. How it would feel to lose you so quickly after you made me love you."

Adrenaline ripped through her nervous system, terminating in an almost painful jolt in her fingertips, like a bolt of electricity. *"What?"*

He carried on, as though he hadn't heard her.

"Christ, I felt like I'd stepped out onto a fucking ledge at twenty stories, and everything was whirling underneath me. I lashed out. I'm sorry."

"You can't."

"Can't what?"

"Love me!" God, what possessed him to say *that*? "Craig, we don't even know one another."

"I'd say we know each other better than some couples ever do."

She blushed. "That was sex."

His eyes glinted. "It sure as hell was. But sex like that ... Nita, that doesn't just happen between strangers. And I've had enough sex with beautiful strangers over the past fifteen years to know the difference. It takes a certain level of trust. It takes an intuitive knowledge of the other."

"That's crazy! We hadn't even had a date prior to jumping in bed."

"What have we been doing the past three years but getting to know each other? We've been measuring each other over these cases. Searching for each other's weaknesses, admiring strengths."

"But I do that with everyone I put on the stand."

"Yeah, but you don't look at anyone else the way you look at me. You don't think about anyone else the way you think about me. And thank God, you didn't call anyone else when you thought you were dying and needed to grab at life. You called *me*, dammit. Me."

Nita did the only thing she could do. She burst into tears.

Chapter 7

CRAIG'S HEART CONTRACTED AS he watched the tears slide soundlessly down her cheeks.

"Christ, I'm sorry, Nita. I didn't mean to make you cry."

"I'm just tired," she said.

Shit. Of course she was tired. "Let me take you home."

"I really should go back in there." She dabbed at her eyes with a tissue she pulled out of her jacket pocket.

"No one will expect you back today. Besides, I can't have you go in there looking like you went three rounds with a bully. Knopfler would kick my ass."

She snorted. "Yeah, like that could happen."

"Let me take you home," he pressed. "I won't even stay if you don't want me to. You need to catch up on your sleep."

She pulled down the sun visor on her side of the car and checked out her reflection. "Ugh." She flipped the visor back into place. "Okay, take me home."

Before she could change her mind, he started the car and eased out of the parking lot. They didn't speak for the ten-minute trip downtown. Craig eased the car to the curb in front of her brownstone.

"Thank you," she said.

Before he could stop it, the question was out: "Can I come in?"

She gazed at him with eyes that still glistened more than they should.

"I'm not looking for sex," he said quickly. "I just want to make you dinner while you shower and make sure you go to bed as soon as you've eaten."

Her eyes widened. "You want to *mother* me?"

Jesus, she was beautiful, puffy eyes, blotchy face and all. "I want to take care of you. If you get fed up with me, you can tell me to leave and I'll go. You have my word on that."

He saw the struggle plainly on her face. The disciplined career woman in her was clearly telling her to send him on his way. The practical, safe side of her personality was no doubt advising her similarly. But the courageously passionate woman she'd showed him last night prevailed.

"Can you make macaroni and cheese?"

Ah, the ultimate comfort food. "The cheesiest."

"Okay, come on up."

Once inside, he told her to take her time, since the mac and cheese would take an hour from scratch, and she did. Clearly, she'd put the time to good use. When she finally showed herself in the kitchen again, her face bore no evidence of her earlier tears. And this despite the fact she wore no makeup. Or at least, nothing he could discern.

"You look great," he said, pulling out a chair for her at one of the places he'd set at the granite-topped island. He'd thought about setting the dining room table and lighting some low candles, but figured that would smack of romance and seduction, which would only put her on the defensive. What he had in mind tonight was a seduction of an entirely different kind. And the warm kitchen was just the spot for it.

"I made tea," he said.

"Really?" He gaze flew to the counter where her teapot sat. "Herbal or black?"

"Some herbal stuff I found. Since the objective is to pack you off to sleep, I didn't figure you needed the caffeine. But I can make black tea if you'd like ... ."

"No, that's perfect."

"Why don't you pour for both of us, then, while I get supper out of the oven."

While she poured the tea, he removed the bubbling macaroni from the oven and dished up two servings.

She wasted no time tasting hers. "Oh, God, this is heavenly! I can't remember the last time I made this from scratch. I usually resort to the boxed stuff for my fix."

"Me, too, but once in a while I like to make the real thing. When I left for college, I made my mother teach me how to make it so I could feel a little bit closer to home."

She took the bait. "College, huh? Where'd you go, and what did you study."

An hour later, they'd both had seconds of both macaroni and tea. And they each knew a lot more about the other than they had when they'd sat down.

When he caught Nita yawning, he apologized. "God, look at me keeping you up. You should be in bed already. I'll just stick these dishes in the dishwasher and take off so you can lock up after me."

He gathered up the dishes and turned toward the dishwasher.

"Craig?"

He put the dishes down and turned back, his face scrupulously blank. "Yeah?"

"I'm sorry I made this so … weird." She lifted a shoulder in an awkward shrug. "I called you, then I jumped on you, and we had last night, and now it's all backwards."

"I'm not sorry," he said roughly. "Because if it hadn't happened like that, it probably wouldn't have happened at all. The only thing that could make me sorry is if I do something now to blow it. Which is why I think I should leave."

She smiled. "You're not blowing it."

He lifted an eyebrow. "No?"

"No." Her face sobered. "Did you mean it earlier? About … you know … feeling like maybe you were falling in love with me?"

"Every word of it."

She frowned. "How can that be?"

"I don't know." He shrugged. "It just *is*. From the moment I first saw your face, I knew you were potential trouble. The kind of trouble I couldn't stay away from. And when you made it clear you were off limits … ."

"You know why I did that. I just couldn't risk getting involved with you. I was afraid it would hurt my practice, my reputation. Maybe even hurt my clients."

"How about now?" He leaned back against the counter. "Are you still afraid that a relationship with me will harm your law practice?"

"I don't know. I mean, I don't believe you'd say or do anything to harm me, but —"

"What if we were married?"

⚜

"Married?" Nita's heart rate, which was already tripping along at a pretty good clip considering the subject matter of their discussion, leapt into hyperdrive.

"Okay, engaged and then married," he allowed. "We could do that, at least, in the right order."

Engaged. Married.

The words bounced around inside her brain. And he was looking at her as though what he'd said were perfectly logical and reasonable. Had he lost his mind?

"But we're not even *dating.*"

"Okay, we can date for a while, then get engaged and married. How's a six-month timetable sound?"

She blinked. "Let me get this straight — you're prepared to *marry me* so we can continue to have sex?"

"No."

"But you just said —"

"I want to marry you because you're the one, Nita. Period." He pinned her with his gaze, fierce and outrageously blue. "I've never felt like this before. I want to lie beside you and just listen to you breathe. When I've had a shitty day, I want to come home to you and lay my head in your lap and feel your hands on my face. And when you've had a shitty day and it feels like one more straw is gonna break your back, I want to be there to carry the load for you. I want you to tell me your darkest fears, and be able to tell you mine."

"My God, Craig." He meant it. He really meant it. Yearning twisted in her gut, sharp and piercing.

"Nita, honey, I've never been able to see my future — *our future* — so clearly. Can't you see it, too? Just a glimmer?"

She *could* see it. All too easily. But could she *have* it? She swallowed. "My father died of a brain tumor at the age of 49."

His brow furrowed. "I'm sorry. That's way too young. But how is that significant?"

"What if it's hereditary?" Suddenly, the fear she'd felt yesterday when Dr. Woodbridge told her she had a brain tumor swelled up again, threatening to spill out in tears. "What if I have a predisposition to the same thing?"

A muscle leapt in his jaw. "Then all the more reason to get on with this courtship, don't you think?"

Oh, Lord, he was wearing her down. Was she really on the verge of accepting his fast track dating/engagement/marriage proposal? Was she brave enough to seize what he offered?

She gnawed the inside of her lip a moment. "What about work?"

"Easy. They've been wanting to rotate me out of major crime and into criminal intelligence for two years now. I've been holding them off because I wasn't ready to quit locking horns with you. I just have to tell the brass I'm ready for a transfer."

She sucked in a breath. He'd given up a sexier, higher-profile assignment to stay in contact with her? A *hostile* her. "You seriously did that?"

"I did. Of course, I gave them completely bogus reasons. They'd have bounced me out of there faster than you can say 'double-chocolate donut' if they'd known the truth."

She blinked rapidly. "What about kids?"

"As in us having them?"

She nodded.

"I'd like a couple, but we're not talking about making *my* body into an incubator. Your body, your call. But if you do want them, I'd happily split the parental leave with you."

"You would not! You'd never live it down with your colleagues, or your employer for that matter."

"My employer wouldn't like it, no, but they're bound by statute. They'd have no choice. And they wouldn't dare take their frustration out on me, because my kick-ass lawyer wife would bring a harassment charge on my behalf."

"Your wife, huh?"

"Well, I certainly hope you're my wife by the time I need that parental leave," he said mildly. "We might have done a few things out of order, but that's one thing I'm old-fashioned enough to want to do right."

She sobered. "Speaking of old-fashioned, I expect fidelity in a partner."

"Good. Because so do I. Even when I'm being a total ass, which I'm told I can be from time to time." He cocked his head to the side. "Did I mention that I'm crazy about you? Yes, I think I did. And we've already demonstrated sexual compatibility . . . ."

She laughed. "You just never let up, do you?"

"Not when I can see my opponent is weakening. You *are* weakening, right?"

She groaned. "God help me, yes. I'm weakening."

His eyes caught fire. "You'll marry me?"

"I'll *date* you," she clarified. "I can't agree to marry a man when I don't even know if he snores. Or leaves the cap off the toothpaste, or his underwear on the floor."

"Don't know, no and no. But fair enough."

Omigod, she'd done it. She'd just committed to a serious relationship with Detective Craig Walker.

So, what was he doing still lounging there against her kitchen counter?

"Craig?"

"Yeah?"

"Aren't you going to . . . I don't know . . . kiss me or something, to seal the deal?"

"Thank you, God!" He was there in a flash, pulling her into a crushing bear hug. "I've been gripping the edge of that damned countertop all this while to remind myself to give you space. I think my fingernails left marks in the granite."

She pulled back to look up at his face, touched by his consideration. "I appreciate your restraint." She slid her arms around his neck and pressed her breasts against his chest. "But no need for it now."

She felt the shudder that passed through him, which made his next words all the more remarkable.

"There's every need for it." He pulled back. "You need sleep, baby. I can't have you go back to work tomorrow even more exhausted than you were today."

She'd known he had a strong protective instinct when it came to women and children; she'd seen in on display on the witness stand many times. But she had no intention of being denied for her own good.

"You're right," she said, lowering her gaze lest he see what she planned. "But won't you lie down with me? I have a feeling that when I wake up, I'm going to need some concrete persuasion that this really happened."

"Now that I can do."

He tipped her chin up and kissed her, his lips incredibly soft and sweet on hers, his big hand impossibly tender. She grasped his face in both hands and kissed him back, then squeaked as he swept her up into his arms.

"Bedtime."

A moment later, he lay on her bed, fully clothed, on top of the covers while she peeled off her clothes. "Aren't you going to undress?"

"Better not."

She stifled a smile at the gruffness of those two words.

"Suit yourself." She walked naked to her dresser and found the skimpiest piece of nightwear she owned, a spaghetti-strapped, gauzy scrap of a nightdress she kept to sleep in when the heat waves of August struck the city. She pulled it over her head, shivering as the sheer cotton batiste settled over her curves. It hit her thighs just below hip level. His gaze slid down her body, making her skin tingle just as the brush of the material had.

She let her own gaze skate over his body, fixing on the growing bulge in the front of his pants. "Oh, my."

He laughed. "You were never planning on sleeping, were you?"

She grinned back. "Not for a while yet."

"You win." He opened his arms. "Come here."

She paused a moment, drinking in his sprawling, powerful body, his open arms, his craggy, overly masculine face. *Mine*, she marveled. Not for a night. Not for a month. For keeps.

"Are you waiting for a pretty please?"

"It couldn't hurt."

"Then pretty please, lover. Come to me."

Barely able to contain the bubble of joy in her chest, she pounced on him, laughing. He grunted as he caught her, but absorbed her weight easily.

She pushed herself to her knees, straddling him.

"Gee, you don't seem at all tired," he observed.

"Not at all." She bent to kiss him, and he slid his hands up her back, his palms hard and urgent, yet tender. "In fact, why don't you let me do all the work? We never did get around to that last night. It was going to be next if I hadn't fallen asleep."

He laughed. "Baby, last night it would have *had* to have been next. You wore me out."

"Mmmmm." She squirmed lower, bringing her bare sex into contact with his erection, straining beneath his clothing. "You seem to have recovered."

"It's a miracle." He reached up to cup her breasts.

It was a miracle, she thought. Miraculous that he loved her. Miraculous that she was poised on the brink of taking that tumble herself.

"Well, if you're going to do all the work, you can start by digging a condom out of my left front pocket. Unless you've already made up your mind about the kids or no kids thing?"

"No way. I don't even know if you snore yet, remember?" She rolled off him, slid her hand in his pocket and came out with a condom. "I know I said I'd do all the work, but I don't think I can get you out of those clothes without your cooperation. You're too big."

"Oh, baby, I'll cooperate."

In ten seconds flat, he was naked and flat on his back in the middle of her bed. She stood there a moment, holding her breath. Fully engorged, his cock nudged his flat, muscled stomach. She let out the breath she'd been holding. "At any time last night, did I mention how wet I get at the sight of that?"

His erection jerked as though she'd physically stroked him.

"Maybe a time or two," he managed.

Smiling, she grasped his member, dragging a sharp inhalation from him as she closed her fingers loosely around him. Then she bent and laid her tongue on the base of his cock, licking it all the way to the tip in one broad, flat stroke.

"Ahhhh!"

Feeling her own internal muscles clenching with excitement, she closed her mouth over his glans and began describing figure eights with her tongue, savoring his salty-sweet taste.

"Nita!" His hands fisted in her hair, holding her head at his groin for long moments as she sucked and licked him like a lollipop. Then he pulled her away. "I think you'd better get that condom on me."

He was right. She needed him inside her. Now. She sheathed him quickly. Straddling him again, she guided the blunt tip of his cock into her slickness. Lowering herself slowly, she savored the sense of fullness as she stretched to accommodate him.

"God, that's good," she said. Balancing herself with her hands on his chest, she rose up again, taking a little more of him on the downswing. As mind-blowing as orgasm was, she loved this just as much, the initial shocking thrill of full penetration. On that thought, she sank the rest of the way, taking his shaft to the root, impaling herself. She cried out with the pleasure of it, and Craig bucked beneath her, grasping her hips and surging up into her.

"No." She flattened her palm on his chest. "Let me."

His hands dropped from her hips to her thighs.

She proceeded to rock herself to orgasm. When she finally stopped spasming around him, she realized he had held himself motionless. Damn, he was still hard, still buried deep inside her!

"Why didn't you come with me?"

"Because I think you can come again."

He sat up, opening his legs and drawing hers up so she sat cradled in his lap, their bodies still joined. The position brought them chest to chest, face to face.

"You are so beautiful," he breathed. "Watching you come like that ... feeling you come like that .... Christ, Nita, I could die happy."

She closed her eyes.

"No, don't baby. Keep your eyes open. I want you to stay with me while we kiss and whisper and fuck."

Something jolted in her chest. He wanted intimacy, not sex. Her throat tightened. "I don't know how to do this."

"Me neither. But why don't we just kiss and whisper and fuck and see what happens."

He slid his hands under her buttocks and rocked into her, even as his lips found hers. It went on forever, caresses and butterfly kisses and nuzzling of ears and whispering of praise. Deep kisses and tender touches and searching of faces with fingertips. And in the midst of it, she felt herself falling.

No, not falling. You couldn't call it falling if you stepped willingly off a cliff. It was terrifying. Exhilarating. Inevitable. When she came again, it was the slowest, longest, most powerful orgasm of her life, and this time, Craig followed.

Chapter 8

CRAIG WOKE UP KNOWING someone was watching him. He opened his eyes to find Nita lying beside him, her head propped on her elbow as she studied his face.

"Morning," he said.

"Good morning."

He glanced at the digital clock on the nightstand. Almost nine o'clock. Good thing he'd wrangled two days off, or he'd be getting chewed out for the second day in a row. "I'm sorry. I fell asleep this time."

"I know. I watched you."

"Do I snore?"

"Not that I noticed. But you do talk in your sleep."

Oh, shit. "I do? What'd I say?"

"I'm going to have to assume you were dreaming about me, with all those *please, babys*."

"That's a safe bet." A lock of hair had fallen forward on her face, and he brushed it back. "So, how's your work schedule? Anything urgent waiting for you?"

"Nothing that won't keep. In fact, I was thinking about playing hooky. But what about you?"

"I'm off until Monday."

She grinned. "Perfect. I'll call in sick." She reached for the phone and started dialing.

He waited until someone had answered, then slid under the sheet. She made a little squeaking noise when she realized he was going down on her, but she didn't fight him.

"Brad?" Her voice came out breathless.

Craig parted her labia and breathed on her tender, exposed sex.

45

"I'm not — aaaah! —"

He smiled as he lapped at her.

"I'm not feeling up to coming in this morning, Brad. I'm going to need the day off."

He closed his mouth around her clitoris and suckled.

"*Yes!* I mean, yes, that's it exactly. Bubonic plaque. Thank you. I'll make it up to you. Bye."

He heard her hang the phone up, then he felt her hands in his hair.

"Come up here!'

He obeyed, slithering up her body with the maximum of friction.

"You realize Brad knows we were making out?"

He grinned. "Honey, I'm pretty sure he would have put that together without my help."

"Yeah, but he knows we were making out *while I was on the phone!*"

"Un-huh." He nuzzled her neck. God, she smelled good. Like the soap from the shower they'd taken before they crashed. Okay, before *he* crashed.

"You're incorrigible."

"I try." He kissed her mouth, and there was silence in the room for a few minutes. When he broke the kiss and started nuzzling his way down her neck, she stopped him.

"Wait! Before you're inside me again giving me mind-blowing orgasms, I need to say something."

He stopped. "What?"

"You know how yesterday you said I was the one?"

His heart tripped, then started to thunder. "Yeah?"

"Well, you're the one for me, too."

Oh, Jesus. "You don't need to say it," he said quickly. "I know you weren't hung up on me the way I was on you, but I'm happy you're giving us a chance. I know I can make you happy, and I think—"

"Oh, for Pete's sake, shut up, will you?" she growled. "I'm trying to tell you that you were the one, right from that first moment. I knew it, but I was too stubborn to act on it. I convinced myself that if I got together with you, I'd be ruined professionally once you got what you wanted. But now I think I was just protecting myself. I was scared. Scared to take a chance. Scared of intimacy with someone I instinctively knew could crush me without even trying. So I took the coward's way out with that 'no cops' rule."

"Are you saying … ?"

"That I love you? Yes. That's exactly what I'm saying. But I didn't want to say it last night. I figured you'd think it was just because you'd given me the most amazing tantric orgasm of my life."

"Say it again!"

"I love you."

"No, the thing about me giving you the best orgasm of your —"

"Craig Walker!" She swatted him.

He responded by pinning her arms above her head.

"Bully." She glared at him.

"Say it again." God, he loved her.

"What? The orgasm thing? Forget it."

"No, the love thing."

She softened beneath him. "I love you, you jerk."

He threw back his head and laughed. "I did warn you I could be an ass."

"I guess you did," she grumbled.

"Can we get married now?"

"No."

"Engaged?"

"Not yet."

"Can we have sex?"

"God, yes."

And once again there was silence in the room.

❧ ❧ ❧

If you enjoyed this free novella, please check out my full-length romantic suspense novels featuring some of the characters you met in this novella. Still very sensual, but a lot more story! Read on for brief samples of the other books in this series, to wit:

Serve and Protect Series
GUARDING SUZANNAH, Book 1
SAVING GRACE, Book 2
PROTECTING PAIGE, Book 3

GUARDING SUZANNAH
Book 1 in the Serve and Protect Series

Product Description

Criminal defense attorney Suzannah Phelps is the bane of the Fredericton police department (they call her She-Rex for her habit of shredding cops in the witness box). She is currently being stalked, but is reluctant to report it to the police, whom she half suspects of being the perpetrators. But when Detective John (Quigg) Quigley learns of it, he's determined to protect her, at considerable risk to his career. They've struck sparks off each other in the courtroom, and he's burning to do the same in the bedroom. When the danger escalates, he has the perfect excuse to pose as her boyfriend, but the closer they get, the more the lines between pretense and reality blur.

Reviews

"Explosively sexy, the chemistry between the two is hot, sensual and sweet all at the same time!"
— *Book Junkie*

"Sizzling chemistry and tingling suspense are combined in GUARDING SUZANNAH to make it the best romantic suspense I've read. I think this award-winning author has produced an edge of your seat beginning to a great series!"
— *The Romance Reviews*

"Quigg harkens back to the hard boiled gum shoes, a tenacious bulldog of a cop .... Suzannah is an upper crust girl who is clearly very used to having her own way. This gives the story an almost modern Noir feel."
— *You Gotta Read Reviews*

"Holy cow - this was an AMAZING read! The twists and turns of this romantic suspense novel had me tied up in knots and hating to put this book aside to sleep!"
— *Marilyn Rondeau, ck2skwipsandkritiques*

Guarding Suzannah (Excerpt)

"Can I give you a hand with that?"

She seemed to just about come out of her skin at his words, whirling to face him. Wide blue eyes locked onto him, and for an instant, Quigg saw fear. Not surprise. Not your garden variety momentary fright when someone startled you. This was real, raw fear. Then it was gone, and she wore her smooth Princess face again.

"Thank you, no. I can manage."

Her voice was cool, polite, completely assured. Had he imagined the blaze of fear?

Bending, she righted the briefcase, deposited it on the car's seat and closed the door. She must have expected him to move on, or at least to step back, because when she turned, she wound up standing considerably closer than before. Closer than was comfortable for her. He could see it in the quick lift of her brows, the slight widening of her eyes. But she didn't step back.

Neither did he.

Damn, she was beautiful. And tall. In those three inch heels that probably cost more than he made in a week, her gaze was level with his. Throw in all that long blond hair that would slide like silk through a man's hands, and a body that would . . . .

"You're that cop."

He blinked. "*That* cop?"

"*Regina vs. Rosneau.*"

"Good memory." They'd secured a conviction on that one, but her client had taken a walk on appeal. Though in truth, Quigg hadn't minded over much. The dirtball had done it, all right, but strictly speaking, the evidence had been a bit thin. One of those fifty/fifty propositions.

"*Regina vs. Haynes.* That was you, too, right?"

Okay, dammit, that one still stung, although the insult was almost two years old now. Two defendants, separate trials, separate representation, each accused managing to convince a jury the other guy'd done it. Of course, Quigg could take consolation from knowing the noose was closing yet again around Ricky Haynes' good-for-nothing drug-dealing neck. Haynes had since moved outside the city limits, beyond municipal jurisdiction, but Quigg had it on good authority that the Mounties were building a rock-solid case against him.

Yes, he could take some consolation in that. Some *small* consolation. Not enough, however, to blunt the slow burn in his gut right now.

"Keep a scrapbook, do you, Ms. Phelps? Or maybe you cut a notch in your little Gucci belt, one for every cop you skewer?"

Something that looked astonishingly like hurt flashed in her eyes, but like before, it was gone before he could be certain he'd really seen it. Then she stepped even closer and smiled, a slow, knowing smile that made him think about skin sliding against skin and sweat-slicked bodies fusing in the dark, and he knew he'd been mistaken. When she extended a slender, ringless finger to trace a circle around a button on his shirt, his heart stumbled, then began to pound.

"Definitely not the belt thing," she said, her voice as husky and honeyed as his most sex-drenched fantasy. "At the rate you guys self-destruct under cross, there'd be nothing left to hold my trousers up, would there, now, John?"

Then she climbed in her gleaming little Beemer and drove off before his hormone-addled brain divorced her words from her manner and realized he'd been dissed.

Against all reason, he laughed. Lord knew it wasn't funny. Certainly, young Langan wouldn't share his mirth.

Of course, the whole thing defied reason, the way it twisted his guts just to look at her. She was rich. She was beautiful. She was sophisticated. She was the daughter of a judge, from a long line of judges. She was ... what? He searched his admittedly limited lexicon for an appropriate term. *Kennedy-esque.*

Meanwhile, his own father had worked in a saw mill; his mother had cleaned other people's houses. Suzannah Phelps was so far out of his league, there wasn't even a real word for it.

She was also the woman not-so-affectionately known around the station house as *She-Rex*. And worse.

Much worse.

Except she hadn't looked much like a She-Rex when she'd spun around to face him, her face all pale and frightened.

Quigg turned and headed for Queen Street, where he'd parked his car. What had spooked her? Not his sudden appearance. He was sure of that. She might not have much use for cops, but she wasn't scared of him.

Maybe it was something inside her car.

He'd reached his own car, which sprouted a yellow parking ticket from beneath the windshield wiper. Great. He glanced up, searching traffic. There she was, at the lights a block away.

What could be in her car to make her look like that? Or was he completely off base? Was it a guilty start, not a frightened start? Hard to say. She'd masked it so quickly.

Damn, he was going to have to follow her.

Climbing into his not-so-shiny Taurus, he fired it up, signaled and pulled into traffic.

Even at this hour with the first of the home-bound traffic leaving the downtown core, tailing her was child's play. As he expected, she headed back to her office. No knocking off early for Suzannah Phelps. She probably put in longer days than he did. Two blocks from her uptown offices, she pulled into another office building's parking lot. Quigg guided his vehicle into the gas bar next door and watched Suzannah drive to the back of the lot where she parked next to a blue dumpster.

Pretending to consult a map he'd pulled from his glove compartment, Quigg watched her get out of the car and scan the lot. Then she circled the BMW, opened the passenger door and pulled something out. The car itself blocked Quigg's view, but he saw a flash of mauvey/pinky floral patterned paper. Then she lifted the dumpster's lid and tossed the object in. Quickly, she rounded the car, climbed in and accelerated out of the lot.

Quigg watched her vehicle travel east along Prospect. When she signaled and turned into her office's parking lot, he slipped his own car into gear. Thirty seconds later, he lifted the lid to the dumpster.

Flowers? She'd been scared witless by flowers?

More likely by who sent the flowers, he reasoned. Maybe they still had a card attached. Out of habit, he patted his pockets for latex gloves before remembering he didn't have any on him. He wasn't on duty. He had some in a first aid kit in his car, but he wasn't about to dig them out. This wasn't an investigation.

Well, not a sanctioned one.

Grimacing, he retrieved the prettily wrapped bouquet with his bare hands. The florist's paper appeared pristine, undisturbed, as though Suzannah hadn't even looked at the contents. Carefully, he peeled the paper back. Then he dropped the bouquet back into the dumpster.

Holy hell! Long-stemmed red roses. Or rather, what he suspected used to be red roses. Now they were more brown than red. Rusty, like old blood. Dead. Probably a dozen of them.

His mind whirled. How had she known? She hadn't even opened the wrapper.

Because it wasn't the first time, obviously.

Because they'd been deposited in her car, right there in the barristers' parking lot, while she was inside defending Leo Warren. While a commissionaire kept an eye on the lot. While her car doors had no doubt been locked.

No wonder she'd been spooked.

He picked up the bouquet again and examined it closer. No card. *There's a surprise, Sherlock.*

Why hadn't she told him? She *knew* he was a cop.

Domestic. The answer came instantly. Had to be. She knew the source, but wasn't prepared to make a complaint because she didn't want to make trouble for the jerk who'd done this, thereby increasing his rage. How many times had he seen that age-old dynamic in operation?

Except he hadn't expected it from Suzannah. She was too much of a fighter. What could be going on in her head?

Quigg tossed the bouquet back in the dumpster and closed the lid. Climbing back into the Taurus, he sat for long moments.

He should leave this alone. He knew it.

He also knew he wasn't going to.

"This, you dumb-ass, is how careers are ruined."

But she'd called him John. Back there, outside the courthouse, she'd called him by his Christian name. Nobody called him John, except his mother. It was *Quigg*, or *Detective Quigley*, or *Officer*, or even *Hey, pig!* But back there, while her index finger had traced delicate circles on his chest, she'd called him John.

Stifling a sigh, he keyed the ignition and slipped the Ford into gear.

SAVING GRACE
Book 2 in the Serve and Protect Series

Product Description

After wrecking her car and waking in hospital with amnesia, fledgling reporter Grace Morgan has no idea why she'd been in the process of leaving the husband she loves so dearly. Her husband, Police Detective Ray (Razor) Morgan tells her she was leaving him for another man, but that just can't be so. Can it? She's determined to remember, even if it kills her. And it just might. When bullets start to fly, Ray is forced to take the wife he believes faithless on the lam until they can figure out who is trying to kill them.

Reviews

"Norah Wilson hits another one out of the park with book two in the Serve and Protect series."
— *The Romance Reviews*

"… a perfect mix of romance and suspense."
— *LoveRomancePassion*

"She (Wilson) combines characters that just jump off the pages, a winning story line and fast action to make this a real page turner."
— *Sugarbeat's Books*

Saving Grace (Excerpt)

BEING DRUNK SLOWED RAY Morgan's reaction time. The telephone managed a full ring before he snatched the receiver.

"Grace?" To his own ears, his voice sounded like someone else's.

A second's silence, then a man's voice. "That you, Razor?"

Ray sagged back into the depths of the couch. John Quigley, from the station.

Not Grace after all. Never again Grace.

"Yeah, it's me." Ray dragged a hand over his face. "'Fraid I'm no good to you tonight, though, Quigg."

Another pause. "You okay, Ray?"

"Sure. Been keeping company with Jim Beam, is all." Ray's lips twisted at his own wit. Okay, so maybe he wasn't that witty, but it was either laugh or cry. "S'okay, though. I'm not catching tonight anyway. Hallett is."

"Just a sec, Ray."

Quigg must have covered the mouthpiece, because Ray could hear muffled conversation in the background.

"Okay, I'm back," Quigley said.

"I was sayin' to call Gord Hallett. He's your man tonight."

"I don't need a detective, Ray. I was looking for you."

"Huh? You're looking for me at, what ... ?" He squinted across the room at the glow of the VCR's digital clock. Grace's VCR. She hadn't slowed down long enough to take anything.

What had he been saying? Oh, yeah, the time. "... eleven o'clock at night?"

"It's Grace."

At the mention of his wife's name, Ray felt the hollowness in his gut open up again, wide and bottomless as ever. Guess the bourbon hadn't filled it after all.

Leave it to Grace to get stopped on her way out of town, in her red Mustang the boys in Patrol had come to know so well. Had she explained why her foot was so heavy tonight? His grip on the phone tightened. Had she told the uniform — a guy Ray would have to face every day for the next ten years — that she was rushing off to meet her lover and couldn't spare the horses?

Her *lover.*

"You got her downtown?" he asked evenly.

"Downtown? Hell, no. They took her to —"

"'Cause you can keep her. You hear me, Quigg? I don't care."

"Dammit, Ray, listen to me. She's been in an accident."

Ray shot to his feet, dragging the telephone off the table. It hit the floor with a crash, but the connection survived. "What happened?"

"She missed a bend on Route 7, rolled her vehicle."

He felt his stomach squeeze. "Is she hurt bad?"

"Hard to say. By the time I got there, they were already loading her into the bus. But she didn't look too bad, considering she rolled that puppy like the Marlboro man rolls a cigarette. Paramedic said he thought she might have lost consciousness for a bit, but she seemed pretty with-it to me."

Wait a minute, Quigg was off duty. Why'd they call Quigg?

Unless Grace was hurt so bad they thought his best friend should break the news.

Ray gripped the receiver so hard now his fingers hurt. "Why'd they call you?"

"Nobody called me. Suz and I were on our way home from visiting friends when we came on the scene. I stopped to see if our Mountie friends could use a hand. When I saw it was Grace, I offered to make the call."

Okay, relax, man. Breathe. Maybe it wasn't that bad. *But she'd rolled the car.*

Pressing a thumb and forefinger to his closed eyelids, he pushed back the images from every bad wreck he'd seen in his twelve years on the force.

"They taking her to the Regional?"

"She's probably there already."

"I'll be there in —" Ah, hell, the booze. *Morgan, you idiot.* "Quigg, I'm in no shape to drive. Can you send a car?"

"Way ahead of you, buddy. Stevie B will be there in about four minutes."

⚜

Four hours later, Ray sat across the desk from Dr. Lawrence Greenfield, the neurologist who'd just finished Grace's workup.

The six cups of coffee he'd downed had sobered him up, but his stomach lining felt like he'd been drinking battery acid.

"So she's going to be okay?" Ray had been through such a wild range of emotions in the five hours since Grace had dropped her bombshell, he didn't know how he felt about this news. Christ, he didn't even know how he was *supposed* to feel. He eyed the doctor, who looked way too young to be fooling around with anyone's grey matter. "She'll walk away with no real injury?"

"I wouldn't go that far. At least not yet. She did suffer a Grade Three concussion." Dr. Greenfield leaned forward in his chair, steepling his hands. "Brain injury is more of a process than an event, Detective. It can escalate over as much as seventy-two hours, so we'll have to wait and watch for the next little while. What I *can* tell you is she has no focal injury we can pinpoint with conventional imaging."

"Focal injury?"

"No concentrated damage in any one area. The scans were clean. On the other hand, any time a patient loses consciousness, we have to be suspicious."

"What do you mean, suspicious?"

"She could have a diffuse injury, where the pathology is spread throughout the brain, rather than focused in a specific spot. We'll have to follow her for a while to rule out more subtle brain injury."

Ray slouched back in his chair, kicking a leg out carelessly. "She's conscious now?"

"Yes. And anxious to see you."

Ray rubbed a hand over the back of his neck. "Then I think I'd go back and look at those scans again, Doc."

"I'm sorry?"

"She can't possibly want to see me." He congratulated himself on how matter-of-fact he sounded. "She left me tonight. She was on her way to join her lover when she had her accident."

Dr. Greenfield blinked. "She told me she was coming home from an interview with a man who raises miniature horses, and that you'd be worried that she was late."

The pony interview? "Doc, that interview was a week ago. The story ran on Monday."

"I see." Dr. Greenfield leaned back. "Well, this puts things in rather a different light."

"What are you saying?"

"I'm saying we could be looking at a retrograde amnesia."

Amnesia? Oh, Christ, he was in a bad novel now. "But you said she'd escaped injury."

"Amnesia can accompany any loss of consciousness, however brief, although I thought we'd ruled it out." Greenfield removed his glasses and polished them. "She identified the date and day."

"Couldn't she have picked that up from the EMTs or the hospital staff?"

"Absolutely. Amnesia victims can be very good at deducing such things from clues gleaned after the accident. But she correctly answered a whole host of other questions for me, including the results of Tuesday's municipal election."

Ray digested this information. "Is it possible she remembers some things, but not others?"

"Oh, yes. In fact, it's quite probable." Dr. Greenfield replaced his glasses. "Amnesia can leave holes in the memory, with no predicting where those holes will appear. The location of the gaps can be as random as the holes in Swiss cheese. In fact, we call it Swiss cheese memory."

Terrific. Freaking wonderful. "So she might remember the election results, but not the fact that she's taken a lover?"

"I suppose it's possible."

To his credit, Greenfield's gaze remained steady, but Ray could read his eyes. Faint embarrassment, carefully masked empathy for the cuckolded husband.

"Or she may not have forgotten Romeo at all, right, Doc?" he rasped. "Just the fact that she told me about him."

"That's also a possibility," the neurologist conceded. "Whatever the case, Detective, I can vouch for the fact that she seems genuinely anxious to see you. She's very much in need of some sympathy and support."

Ray made no comment, keeping his face carefully blank.

"I should add that new memories are especially vulnerable, since it takes a few days for your brain to move them into permanent memory." Dr. Greenfield hunched forward again. "Do you use a computer, Mr. Morgan?"

Ray struggled to follow. "Of course I do. Who doesn't?"

"Well, to make a very crude analogy, fresh events, whatever might have happened in the last couple of days, are to your brain what random-access memory, or RAM, is to your computer. If the computer unexpectedly loses power before a bit of data gets stored on the hard drive, it's lost. You can boot up again, but whatever was in the RAM has been wiped out. Thus, with any loss of consciousness, it's possible to lose memories that were in transition."

Great. She'd probably forgotten she'd dumped him.

Ray stood. "Well, no time like the present, is there, Doc? Let's go see my darling wife."

Dr. Greenfield's eyes widened. "Surely you don't plan to tell her … I mean, you won't —"

"Won't what? Suggest she call her boyfriend so she can cry on his shoulder instead?" Ray drew himself up, growing in height and girth, and let his expression go flat in the way he knew inspired fear. *Bad cop to badder cop.* "Why shouldn't I? She chose *him.*"

Dr. Greenfield looked singularly unintimidated, no doubt because he'd already seen the raw edge of Ray's anguish.

Damn you, Grace, how could you do this to me?

"The fact remains that she seems to need *you* right now. She's quite distraught. The last thing she needs is to be upset any further. If a diagnosis of retrograde amnesia is confirmed, I'd like to give her a chance to recover her memories on her own." Dr. Greenfield's intense gaze bored into Ray. "Can I have your cooperation on that point?"

Ray stared back at the doctor, unblinking. "I hear you, Doc. Now, take me to her."

⁂

Grace Morgan felt like a dog's breakfast.

Despite the painkillers the nurse had given her, everything she owned seemed to hurt, albeit in a distant way, and her head ached with a dull persistence. But she hadn't cried.

In fact, she seemed unable to cry. Instead of tears, there was just a hot, heavy misery in her chest. If only Ray would come. If he were here with her, she could cry rivers.

She'd cry for her beloved Mustang, shockingly crumpled now, a red husk of twisted metal they'd had to open like a sardine can. How had she come out of it alive?

She'd cry for her carelessness.

She'd cry for scaring Ray, and for scaring herself.

Ray. He would gather her close and soothe her while the pain seeped out, soaking his shirt. He would lend her his strength, his toughness. He'd kiss her so carefully and sweetly .... .

She could almost cry, just thinking about it. Almost.

Ray, where are you?

On cue, the door swung open to admit her husband. Her heart lightened at the sight of him, so strong, so solid. His shoulders seemed to fill even this institutional-size doorway.

If she felt bad, he looked worse. Haggard. And for the first time she could remember in the six years she'd known him, he looked positively rumpled, and his face was shadowed with stubble as though he'd missed his second shave of the day.

Poor pet. He must have been so worried.

"Ray." Her right arm hindered by IV lines, she reached across her body with her left arm. He took her hand, but there was something wrong. He looked ... funny. Guarded. Wrong.

Oh, Lord, was she dying after all? Was her brain irrevocably damaged and nobody wanted to tell her? She could be hemorrhaging right now, her brain swelling out of control. Maybe that's why her head hurt. Maybe ....

Then he touched her forehead, brushing aside the fringe of hair peeping out from under the bandage, his gentleness dispelling her crazy impression.

"You all right?"

She would be now. "Yeah, I'm all right. Unless you know something I don't."

That look was back on his face again. "What do you mean?"

"They didn't send you in here to tell me they mixed up the charts, by any chance? That my brain is Jell-O after all?"

He smiled, but it didn't reach his eyes. "No, your head is fine, as far as they can tell."

She drew his hand to her cheek, pressing it there with her own palm. Some of the pain abated. "That's what they told me, too, but you'd never know it from the way I feel."

"Do you remember what happened?"

She swallowed hard, her throat tight with the need to cry. "I rolled the Mustang."

"Like a cowboy's cigarette, to quote Quigg." Another ghost of a smile curved his lips. Lips he hadn't yet pressed to hers.

She smiled tremulously. "I guess I'm lucky, huh?"

"Very lucky."

The tears welled, scalding, ready to spill. "I really loved that car."

"Something tells me you could love another one."

Again that twisting of his lips. It wasn't humor that lit his eyes. What? A vague, formless anxiety rose in her breast.

"A newer model, with fewer miles on the odometer. Or maybe something faster, flashier."

She wasn't imagining things. His tone was … off. What was it she was hearing? Accusation? Grace blinked. "Are you very angry? About the car, I mean?"

He seemed to swallow with difficulty, and his hand tightened on her chin. "Grace, I don't give a damn about the car."

For the first time since he entered the room, she finally saw what she expected to see in his face. *To hell with the car. You're okay. You're safe*, his eyes said. Her sense of strangeness dissipated.

"I was so scared."

He pulled her into his arms. The dam broke and her tears spilled over at last.

⁂

They kept Grace overnight for observation.

Ray stayed, planting himself in the single chair by her bed. Once he dozed off, waking when the night nurse came in for yet another check. At eight o'clock, he left Grace to her breakfast and went down to the lobby to find a pay phone.

He was a fool, plain and simple. He knew it, but knowing didn't seem to help. He was going to take her home anyway.

Of course, it wasn't like he had a helluva lot of alternatives. He couldn't send her home to her mother, that frozen excuse for a human being, even supposing Elizabeth Dempsey would take her daughter in. Grace's father had died two years ago, completing the retreat from an imperious wife which Ray figured must have begun minutes after Grace's conception.

No, there was no place for Grace to go. Not in her current condition.

Ray dropped his quarter and punched in the number, kneading the tense muscles at the back of his neck as he waited for his Sergeant to answer. It was likely to be a short-lived arrangement anyway, having Grace back home. When she didn't show up for her rendezvous, no doubt lover boy would come looking —

"Quigley."

"Quigg, it's me."

"About time you checked in. How's it going?"

"Grace is good. Concussed and sore as hell, but okay."

"Yeah, I've been getting regular updates. But that's not what I meant."

Ray bit back a sigh. "Is this where I'm supposed to ask what you *did* mean?"

"Last night you were ready to let her rot in the lockup."

"What's wrong with that?" Pain shot up to the base of his skull, and Ray massaged his neck again. "Biggest favor I could do for the motoring public, with that lead foot of hers."

"Except you don't know how to be mean to Grace. Leastways, not before yesterday."

"Yeah, well." Ray rubbed at a scuff on the tiled floor with the toe of his Nikes. There was a pause at the other end of the line, no doubt so Quigg could digest that pithy comment.

"I think you should take some time off," Quigg said at last.

"That's actually why I'm calling. I'll need a day or so to get Grace settled."

"I was thinking more in terms of weeks."

"Weeks?" The idea of spending days at home with Grace as she recovered her mobility — and her memory — filled him with cold dread. Not that it would take long. Even if nature didn't cooperate, Grace's paramour was bound to show up to hurry the process. Ray had been counting on putting in long days on the job, both before and after Grace's veil of forgetfulness fell — or was ripped — away.

"I can't take time off. You'll be short-staffed."

"Not for long. Woods is three days away from rotating in."

"He'll need orientation .... "

"He's been here before," Quigg said. "Couple of days, it'll be like he's never been gone."

"But what about Landis?"

"I'm pretty sure our small-town bad guy will be here when you get back."

"There's nothing small-town about that bastard, and you know it." Ray knew he was letting the simmering fury of his domestic disaster leach into his voice, but he didn't care. That puke Viktor Landis was a worthy target for it. "He's got his fingers into every dirty deal that goes down in this town."

"And some day you'll catch him at it, but not this week. And not next week." Quigg's agreeable tone turned hard. "Compassionate leave, Razor. Two weeks, starting now. The work'll be here when you get back. It's not going anywhere."

"But I only need a few days, not weeks."

"Take 'em anyway."

A definite command. Ray gripped the receiver tightly. Dammit, how could his friend do this to him? He *needed* to work.

"Get away from the station house," Quigg said, his voice softer now. "Spend some time with Grace. Chrissakes, Ray, you haven't taken a real break since your honeymoon."

Quigg's words stopped the retort on Ray's tongue. Had it been that long since he'd taken a vacation? He was passionate about his job, but *four years?* Why hadn't Grace said something?

"What do you say, buddy? You gonna take the time or do I have to suspend you?"

Before his promotion last year, Quigg had worked right alongside Ray in the detective bureau. Hell, he was the best friend Ray had in the world. But it wasn't going to make any difference here. Quigg meant business.

Ray put his hand on the phone's switch hook, ready to break the connection. "A week."

"Two." Another command. "And Ray? I know you're not in the market for unsolicited advice, but I'm gonna give you some anyway. Whatever you need to do to get straight with Grace, do it. She's a keeper."

"You're right."

"Of course I'm right. She's a good —"

"I meant about the unsolicited advice." With that, he replaced the receiver.

He stood staring at the telephone for a few minutes. Then, feeling like a man condemned, he turned on his heel and went in search of the doctor to see about Grace's discharge.

PROTECTING PAIGE
Book 3 in the Serve and Protect Series

Product Description

Single parent Paige Harmer is at her wit's end about her son. Dillon's a good kid, but he's fallen in with a bad crowd. She's determined to enlist the help of her next door neighbor, the extremely handsome and much younger Tommy Godsoe. Tommy is a local cop, and until he got shot recently in a police raid, was a dog handler. His injury is such that he can never go back to field work, and he refuses to be a desk jockey. All he wants is to nurse his wounds in solitude, and he's done a great job driving his friends and colleagues away. But Paige is an unstoppable force. Before he knows it, he's drawn into their lives. As it turns out, Paige and Dillon are going to need a cop in their corner. And Tommy needs Paige to drag him out of his self-pity and back to life.

Reviews

"This delightful and sensual romance is gritty and real. Protecting Paige combines tension-filled action, humor and great writing to produce this amazingly tender romance."
— *The Romance Reviews*

"Norah Wilson has another winner in this book."
— *LoveRomancePassion*

"Norah has a talent when it comes to consistently delivering heroines that readers can relate to."
— *MaldivianBookReviewer*

"What can I say? Norah has done it again. I think this may be my favorite in the Serve and Protect series."
— *Redheads Review it Better*

Protecting Paige (Excerpt)

CONSTABLE TOMMY GODSOE'S BLOOD sang.

His breath rasped harshly in his ears as he pelted along the concrete sidewalk, but he wasn't winded. Not yet. Not even close. Max, the four-year-old Belgian Malinois straining at the business end of the thirty-foot lead, lent Tommy extra speed. Even now, backup was falling further and further behind, but Tommy couldn't check Max's momentum or the dog would think he was being corrected.

Suddenly, at the mouth of an alleyway, Max slowed. Without conscious thought, Tommy took up the slack in the lead even as he studied the dog nosing the asphalt. The dog wheeled in a tight semi-circle, then turned away from the alley and shot off again down the sidewalk. Tommy fixed the location in his mind. Max had eliminated the alleyway as a direction of travel. Always had to remember the last negative sign. If they lost the trail further on up ahead, they could come back to this spot, so Max could pick up the scent again.

At the next alleyway, Max did the same check, but this time he bounded off down the narrow passageway. Tommy raced after him, his heart rate kicking up another notch.

Fence!

Max cleared it in one leap, and Tommy vaulted over it right behind him. Over the sound of his own breathing, he heard backup in the mouth of the alley now. Good. No need to radio his location. He could save his breath for —

Ding-*dong.*

What the hell?

Tommy jerked awake, struggling up into a sitting position. The sheets, cool with sweat, pooled in his lap, and his heart pounded against his ribs as though he'd run a marathon.

Ah, Jesus wept. A dream. It was just a dream. He wasn't a cop anymore. He wasn't a dog handler. Bitterness, familiar as the pain in his hip, curdled his stomach.

A light tapping at his door.

"All right, all right, keep your shirt on."

Throwing off the sheet, he swung his legs gingerly over the edge of the bed. He thought about scooping up the blue sweat pants from the floor and hauling them on over his boxers, but another peal of the doorbell dissuaded him. Grabbing his cane, he lurched to his feet and hobbled toward the living room, grimacing with every step.

Ding-*dong.*

Cripes, that's what his doorbell sounded like? Something from a 50s Avon commercial? He'd lived here four years and couldn't remember ever hearing his own doorbell. No doubt the 'Beware of Dog' sign had something to do with that. He and Max never stayed indoors when they could be outside, and they sure as hell never waited around for life to come to them.

Until now.

The doorbell sounded again, and he wished he still had his service weapon. He'd happily put a round into that little speaker by the front door.

Reaching the door at last, he tore it open. *"What?"*

⋄⋇⋄

Paige Harmer took an instinctive step backward.

When she'd moved into this duplex last month, the other side had been vacant. The landlady'd said its occupant was in hospital recovering from surgery. But even after her neighbor had come home nearly two weeks ago, the unit next door had been unnaturally quiet. No visitors came or went, and no music thrummed through those walls. If it weren't for the small bag of garbage that materialized at the curb beside hers every Tuesday morning, and the occasional muted sound of a television deep in the night, she'd have sworn the other apartment was deserted. Now, her neighbor stood framed in the doorway, wearing a pair of white boxers and a thunderous expression.

And oh, Christmas, he was most gorgeous thing she'd clapped eyes on in years, outside of a Calvin Klein ad.

Despite their current storminess, his eyes were blue as the July sky. Black hair, a startling contrast to his pale complexion, stood up in all directions, all the sexier for its dishevelment. Thick, black eyebrows slanted over those killer eyes. More dark hair crowned his chest in a liberal thatch, tapering to a thin line that arrowed out of sight beneath his boxers.

Runner, she thought. *Endurance athlete.* Just a hair over average height, with a leanness that shaded toward too thin. Yet the conformation of arms and chest disclosed enough wiry muscle to give the impression of power.

"Can I help you?"

Mister, if you can't, there's no help for me.

The thought barely had a chance to form before her internal censor roared to life. He was way too young for her to be ogling, for goodness sake. *Hardly much older than Dillon, by the look of him.*

There, that did it. Though he was clearly nowhere near as young as her son, the mental association was enough to clamp a firm leash on her imagination.

Unfortunately, the extra seconds it took to channel her thoughts in more pure directions didn't go unnoticed. One thick eyebrow arched inquiringly, reminding her she hadn't yet stated her purpose.

She felt a flush begin to climb her neck. No chance he'd miss that, either. Her skin was almost translucent, at least the stuff between the freckles. She lifted the foil-wrapped plate she held. "I thought you might like some dinner."

He looked at the plate. "Thanks, but I'm not a big eater."

"I can see that," she said, injecting her tone with the same censorious note she might use with her son when he ignored his body's nutritional needs. He shifted, and she finally noticed the cane, which he appeared to be leaning on pretty heavily. "Don't worry. It'll freeze nicely if you can't handle it all right now."

"Look, lady, that's real nice of you, but —"

"I'll just put it in the refrigerator for you, shall I?"

She angled sideways and slipped right past him before he could finish brushing her off. No way was she going back to her lonely unit to worry about Dillon. Not tonight.

"That way, I presume?" She indicated the direction the kitchen must be, if the place were laid out in the mirror image of hers.

"Uh … yeah."

Seconds later, Paige stood in front of a white dinosaur of a refrigerator, a twin to the one that rattled and hummed in her own kitchen, right beside the commercial refrigeration unit she'd installed for her business. That's where the similarity ended, she discovered, as she opened the refrigerator's door.

Five bottles of beer, domestic. Some Chinese takeout cartons that bulged ominously as though approaching an explosive state. A drying chunk of cheddar cheese, circa 2008. A few bottles of condiments. No eggs, no dairy, no vegetables, no fruit.

Hearing him arrive at the kitchen door — the thumping of the cane on the linoleum-covered floor announced his progress — she glanced over at him.

"Is this the part where you tell me you're really one of the undead and have no need of sustenance beyond human blood?"

He didn't smile. If anything, he scowled more fiercely. "I've been meaning to get to the grocery store."

"It must be hard."

He followed the drift of her gaze. She could tell by the way his hand tightened on the cane's handle.

His jaw hardened even further, if possible. "I manage."

"Are you hungry? The food's still hot." She waggled the foil-wrapped plate temptingly. "Stuffed pork chops with mashed potatoes, glazed carrots and gingered parsnips."

"It's okay," he said, after a split-second hesitation. "You can just put it in the fridge."

Fat chance. She'd caught the fleeting look of indecision in his eye as she'd described what was under the foil. He was hungry, all right. "Aw, come on, sit down and eat. I need the distraction."

Those cigar-thick eyebrows soared. "You want to stay and watch me *eat*?"

"Relax, fella. Nothing kinky. I just don't want to go back over there yet. I've done two loads of laundry, vacuumed the carpet within an inch of its life, baked three cheese cakes and seven pies. I have nowhere to put any more baking and nothing left to clean. So if I go home now, I've got nothing left to do but worry about Dillon."

"Who's Dillon?"

Ah! A question. And she hadn't even dragged it out of him. That was an improvement. "My son."

"Where is he?"

She blew out her breath, lifting a strand of auburn hair off her face. "If I knew that, I wouldn't be worried, would I? Or maybe I would, at that," she amended, thinking about the hard-looking young man Dillon had been hanging with lately.

"He's missing?"

The sharpness of his tone drew her glance to his face. His eyebrows were drawn together again in a frown.

She shrugged. "He's seventeen, almost eighteen. I can hardly describe him as missing every time he slams out of the house in a foul mood."

That surprised him. She could see him doing the mental arithmetic, calculating her minimum age. *That's right, son. Old enough to be your mother, even if I don't look it.*

Okay, that was an exaggeration. A huge exaggeration. But older than him by quite a few years, she'd wager.

"Sit." She pulled a tea towel off the oven door handle where it had been hung to dry after its last use and flopped it on the table as an impromptu place mat, then plunked the plate down on it. "I nuked the ceramic plate before dishing up the food so it would stay nice and warm."

"I don't even know your name."

Way to go, Paige. Barge in and take over the man's life without an introduction.

"Sorry." She wiped her right hand on her jeans and extended it. "Paige Harmer. Your new neighbor."

She regretted her gesture immediately, as he had to lurch forward to grasp her hand. He didn't grimace, but she could feel the tension in his grip. Pain.

"Tom Godsoe."

"I know." At his enquiring look, she hastened to add, "Mrs. Graham mentioned your name."

Paige had been impressed at how close-mouthed her landlady had been about her tenant's private life. As a prospective new tenant, all Paige had needed to know was that her neighbor wasn't a creepazoid. She'd found her landlady's discretion commendable at the time, but now she couldn't help but wish the other woman had been a little less discreet. For instance, what did Tom Godsoe do for a living? How had he sustained the injury that made crossing a room the grueling ordeal it appeared to be?

"Okay," he said at last, "if I'm going to have an audience, I think I'd better get dressed."

Not on my account.

Before something like that escaped her mouth, she averted her eyes from those square shoulders and lightly-muscled expanse of chest. "Take your time. I think I spotted some coffee beans and a grinder. I'll just brew us a pot of java."

"Be my guest," he drawled, then turned and thumped away.

A smile tugging at her lips, Paige reached for the gourmet coffee beans.

Also available from Norah Wilson:

Sensual Romantic Suspense w/ Paranormal Element
EVERY BREATH SHE TAKES (coming 6/19/12 from Montlake
Romance)

Sensual Paranormal Romance
THE MERZETTI EFFECT: A Vampire Romance
NIGHTFALL: A Vampire Romance

As N.L. Wilson
(writing partnership of Norah Wilson and Heather Doherty)
Dix Dodd mysteries (humorous)
**THE CASE OF THE FLASHING FASHION QUEEN:
FAMILY JEWELS**
DEATH BY CUDDLE CLUB (coming soon)

As Wilson Doherty
(writing partnership of Norah Wilson and Heather Doherty)
YA Paranormal
THE SUMMONING: Book 1 in the Gatekeepers Series
ASHLYN'S RADIO

About the Author

Norah Wilson lives in Fredericton, New Brunswick with her husband, two adult children, her beloved Lab-Rottweiler mix Chloe, and numerous rats (the pet kind). Norah has had three of her romantic suspense stories final in the Romance Writers of America's Golden Heart® contest until she sold her first story in 2004. She was also the winner of Dorchester Publishing's New Voice in Romance contest in 2003.

Norah loves to hear from readers!

Connect with Her Online:
Twitter: http://twitter.com/norah_wilson
Facebook: http://www.facebook.com/#!/profile.php?id=1053773212
Norah's Website: http://www.norahwilsonwrites.com
Wilson Doherty's Website: http://www.writersgrimoire.com

20319405R00049

Made in the USA
Charleston, SC
07 July 2013